THE NOVICES OF LERNA

Ángel Bonomini

Translated from the Spanish by
Jordan Landsman

**TRANSIT
BOOKS**

Published by Transit Books
1250 Addison St #103, Berkeley, CA 94702
www.transitbooks.org

Translation copyright © Jordan Landsman, 2024
ISBN: 978-1-945492-85-3 (paperback)
Cover design by Sarah Schulte | Typesetting by Justin Carder
Printed in the United States of America

9 8 7 6 5 4 3 2 1

 This project is supported in part by a grant from the National
Endowment for the Arts.

THE NOVICES OF LERNA

THE NOVICES OF LERNA

THE MONTH I GRADUATED from university (and not exactly with flying colors), the editor of the alumni magazine asked if I would do him a big gauchada. He wanted me to write him an article. Since I didn't know how to say no, I delivered a few modest pages, mostly class notes mixed with an abundance of quotes. That was my entire academic record: a degree I had barely obtained and an article of dubious originality.

With such a meager résumé, I couldn't help but be surprised when, a few weeks after my article was published, I received a proposal from the University of Lerna: they were offering me a six-month fellowship. What was even more astonishing was that they required (along with my confirmation) a frankly disconcerting report of my physical characteristics.

Yes, the fellowship was tempting in and of itself: lots of money, the unilateral ability (on my part) to rescind the agreement at any time, paid travel, paid clothing, life insurance, the possibility of taking classes in my field as well as others, not a single subsequent obligation (publications or reports); a true sinecure that would also give me the opportunity to see the world.

But in addition to the unexpected offer and unusual requests, there was something else I found unnerving: the tone in which the letter from Lerna was written. The syntax was generally unobjectionable, but the tone aroused my suspicion due to how cloying, cautious, and bland it was. An example: "Illustrious Doctor Beltra: The humble and traditional University of Lerna, dedicated, as your Eminence is not unaware, to legal studies and the social sciences for more than two centuries, contacts you, the Eminent Doctor, by way of this humble servant (the letter was from the rector) so that you might have the generosity to . . ." As you can see, the university was extremely humble, the rector a servant, and I was illustrious and eminent. My porteño nature could not help but suspect that this was a joke orchestrated by some maula who fancied himself a humorist. I went to the Swiss embassy, where I was put in contact with someone named Curelli who, mysteriously, already knew who I was. What's more, he had copies of the letters they had sent me from Lerna, which formed part of a voluminous dossier labeled with my name. Intrigued, I tried to find out what the hell was in this monstrous compendium, but the attaché Curelli—the fourth or fifth in the embassy vaguely dedicated to "cultural information and affairs"—categorically refused to let me see it (and he was not very polite about it, either). My experience at the embassy, although briefly disturbed by this promptly forgotten incident, achieved its goal: it dispelled my suspicion that the invitation was the work of some jokester.

And so, I wrote to Lerna to communicate my acceptance "in principle" and to announce that I would send them their copious forms as soon as I had them ready. To this letter, I received a reply dripping with syrup, written so mawkishly that it wasn't just cloying but actually repugnant.

I knew at once I would need help filling out my "physical information" on the questionnaire. It was impossible to take the requested measurements without someone's aid, and it would be difficult to convince anyone that I wasn't filling out the application for an insane asylum. For example, I had to provide the measurements of my biceps when they were hanging by my side as well as completely flexed. When we were younger, I had struck the same pose in front of my cousin Lisandro to prove that I was stronger than him. Therefore, it was Lisandro himself to whom I turned for help. The measurements were so detailed and varied that someone could have easily reproduced my body down to the millimeter. The form was seven pages long, each one brimming with checkboxes.

The photographs (the cost of which was covered by the university) demanded a greater exercise of patience and will. Believe me when I say that the sacrifice they entailed nearly dissuaded me from the trip. They required such an exhaustive survey, so to speak, of my poor body that by the end I was stripping off more than decorum permits. It was my sense of humor and Lisandro that got me through it. My cousin photographed me partially and totally and from every angle imaginable. The delivery of these materials to Europe was handled by the fourth (or fifth) attaché at the embassy, who had also provided us with cameras, film, lenses, lights, and many other gadgets.

A few days after I finished the mountain of paperwork, I received another letter, this one markedly unpleasant. It seemed I was Lerna's ideal candidate. The rector, deans, department heads, and a whole string of authorities affirmed and signed and stamped a declaration that congratulated themselves and me for a "happy end to the negotiations." In the same envelope was a check that somewhat alleviated the stupidity of the letter. My flight was scheduled for the first Monday of December.

Lisandro, kindhearted as ever, strove to dissipate my growing concerns. How could I pass up this opportunity? My abnegation had to do with the humiliating nature of their requests. But to Lisandro they were just examples of the watchmaker's spirit so typical of the Swiss. Watchmakers or not, they had managed with their gloved and affected means—to which I am so hostile—to put me between a rock and a hard place.

The end of October came, and I had to resign my position at the court (or ask for a leave of absence) if I wanted to travel on the date set by Lerna. Resigning was out of the question. I knew my leave would be granted automatically for a fellowship like this, but I asked with the secret hope that it would be denied. Judge Riera, who has known me since I was a child, was so moved when he read my request that he almost cried.

I felt like I was being ambushed. As a rule, a porteño is reluctant to abandon his neck of the woods. I spoke with Lisandro about Lerna until he was bored out of his mind. I went over the facts. The Swiss are Swiss and there was no reason to be surprised by their strangeness. Accepting the invitation would bring me the following benefits: a guaranteed promotion when I got back, the chance to disentangle myself from a few women who were beginning to complicate my life, an economic solution for the next few years if I reconciled myself to saving a little bit of the large quantity of money provided by the fellowship, a visit to Europe, and, as Judge Riera put it, "the incredible opportunity to move away from one's country and see it with the double perspective of time and distance." Personally, I couldn't care less about the latter, but considering the scarcity of favorable elements to tip the scales toward accepting, I opted to consider it. The prospect of being promoted didn't move me either: I know full well that it's best to limit oneself to a tiny position in order to live in peace. To become the registrar, the manager, the chief, is to make the same deal as the toad who traded his eyes for a tail: goodbye to drinking two glasses too many, goodbye to staying up late reading, goodbye to friends, goodbye to women. The part about the women had its advantages, but I couldn't help being upset by this "imposed" separation and, perhaps most importantly, having to abandon the conflicts that dating more than one woman simultaneously implied. Visiting Europe is something that every Argentine keeps in reserve as an unquestionable inheritance; going there is almost a disappointment. The economic solution was a bit questionable; there was no need to solve something that wasn't a problem for me. I always felt saving money was useless. I don't have the capacity or the need to save. I spend what I earn and, no matter how little it is, it's always enough.

In addition to all this, as I already mentioned, I didn't deserve a fellowship. I hadn't asked for one. The application process made me suspicious. The tone of the negotiations was highly disagreeable, and, in an imprecise but unavoidable way, the entire thing inspired in me a sharp annoyance, an uncontrollable distrust.

However, as if a foreign will were exercising itself over my decisions, I embarked (to be precise, I took a plane) on the date indicated by Lerna. At that point, my experience in the air had not exceeded four hundred miles: a one-way trip to Córdoba. (On the return trip, I traded the flight for a bus ride.)

I must confess that my flight to Europe was very enjoyable. I fell in love with a flight attendant (Sandra), and we had the good fortune that certain mechanical breakdowns delayed the flight for thirty-eight hours in Lisbon. My ticket gave me the choice of taking another flight to Geneva or waiting in Portugal. I stayed. Sandra would fly out of Portugal, but we now had one day and two nights ahead of us.

Oh, how I was later nursed by the memories of that young lady during my solitude at Lerna! I had no idea of the importance these few Portuguese hours would have in my future. We spent almost the entire time in a small hotel whose railings and windows were reminiscent of the decor that amateur theaters use to portray the peninsula. Sandra was very warm. She was very sweet. For my own part, I knew that I had to act economically, that is to say, to capitalize on that skin, those eyes, that voice, because it would be a while before I encountered them again. I'll admit it was with a utilitarian sense that I looked at her teeth and smile, as I tried to fix in my mind her ordinary gestures and casual remarks. I wasn't going to see her again for six months and so I let her enter my memory like an army of details whose aim was to invade and occupy me, but in which I would find my nourishment. I thought to myself, "I'm falling in love voluntarily." Later, in Lerna, I would make a daily, meticulous consumption of that premeditated stockpile. On occasion, I had to attend to that abundance of health and beauty just to restore my sanity.

I arrived in Geneva the afternoon of December 7. Separating myself from Sandra was hard. I found the city horrible: a sort of public relations office where what's on the surface just barely disguises the hidden truth.

On Sandra's recommendation, I took a room in the Hotel Krasnopolsky, which she had visited during her travels. The idea that she had been there—in perhaps the same room I was staying in—made me happy. I imagined her moving around from one side of the room to the other. Lying on the bed, not thinking about Lerna at all, I retrieved every moment I spent in Lisbon and, in some cases, corrected past situations in my mind to improve the memories.

At noon the following day, I had to take a train to Umsk, the nearest town to the university. I went out that night to eat and afterward slipped into a movie theater that was showing a western. My memories of Sandra were weighing too heavily upon me. I slept poorly my first night in Switzerland. I ate breakfast late and left directly for the train station. During the trip, overcome by fatigue, worked up by the plane, by Sandra, by our goodbye, and by Geneva, and facing the prospect of having to meet new people, I navigated extravagant half dreams with the foggy image of Sandra in the ever-present background.

I got off at the dark and deserted platform in Umsk. My only luggage was a suitcase. Once the train had left, I tried to make my way with the insufficient help of a few pale streetlights. The area was mountainous and heavily wooded, surely a typical one-horse mountain town, and at that hour of the wintry afternoon the people tucked themselves into their houses. I thought it would be unobjectionably clean, the gardens cared for to a depressing degree. There would be traffic lights even though drivers were respectful of transit laws to the point of religiosity.

I was having these thoughts when I saw a man wearing a pale-blue jumpsuit walking toward me. His gait was elastic and above all very quiet because, evidently, he was wearing rubber-soled shoes. Despite the weakness of the light, my surprise increased as he walked over. When he said, "Good afternoon, Dr. Beltra," I nearly fainted. Was I speaking, or was he? "I'm Gonçalves, an engineer by trade. I've come from Lerna to pick you up." The scene was dreamlike, but reality made it exaggerated. My own voice, my expressions, my face, were coming from another person and directed at the inanimate stone to which I had been converted. Gonçalves added that he was Portuguese and that he was one of the fellows invited by Lerna. I registered this information in a very confused way because, instead of listening, I was completely focused on his appearance. How could I cross the Atlantic, fall in love with a woman, sleep in foreign countries, and, after an exhausting train ride, arrive somewhere new only to realize I wasn't myself anymore? How could I be this benevolent Portuguese engineer, coming to pick me up and bring me to a legendary university? Gonçalves's silence gave me time to contemplate the horrifying possibility of my own depersonalization, and perhaps even my own death, which may have already occurred without my having accepted it.

"I know we look very similar," he said suddenly, as if he were reading from a script. "It's precisely for that reason that we're here. Furthermore, as I will soon explain, we're not the only ones. There are twenty-four fellows and we're all identical." When I finally snapped out of my stupor and put out my hand to confirm that both of us were alive, I began breathing normally. But I had to make an enormous effort to speak. "Wait a second," I said. "This requires an explanation. And if possible, at a bar, with a whiskey in front of me." The man agreed. "The same thing happened to all of us. This isn't the first time I've come to pick up one of the fellows." He took my luggage and walked toward the exit of the platform. A Swiss in uniform (I don't know if he was a policeman or a railroad employee) greeted us courteously as we passed. We got into a small car that was very warm. "Finding out you have a twin, at my age . . ." I said as if not speaking to Gonçalves. "It's even more surprising to find out you have twenty-four twins," replied the engineer.

I sat next to him in the car but avoided looking at him out of discretion. But after a while I couldn't resist the temptation to observe his mannerisms. He was absolutely identical to me. What's more, as I watched him closely, I discovered several details that corresponded to me but that, of course, I had never seen in my own face. Seeing one's own mouth smiling, one's own eyes looking (but not in a dream, right there, a foot and a half away); to see one's identity moved, displaced onto another person that in some sense is oneself: I felt a wave of hatred, and it seemed to me the theft was of a different magnitude than the one I had until then granted it. In a very concrete way, I realized I was capable of killing this man. Insofar as he was himself, I didn't make any sense: he denied me the simple and rudimentary grounds for feeling like myself. I understood that when he smiled my smile, he was stealing my doubts, usurping my anguish, squandering my happiness, putting himself in Sandra's eyes and my parents' graves, sweeping away my past, and crushing my future. And so, as if I were a little drunk, I said to him in a voice that trembled but was full of import, "I am Ramón Beltra." And he, speaking as though he were strengthened by the security of his disdain or the annoyance of his fatigue, replied, "Yes, and I am Julián Gonçalves."

But a few blocks away, I was invaded by another wave of something like compassion. I thought about how his heart was pumping with blood just like mine, how he must have gone through the same childhood anguishes, experienced the same pain, mourned the same deaths. He'd felt the same emotions that I had over the course of twenty-four years of life. But the strange thing was that my life, which had been tolerable, and even somewhat pleasurable, seemed too painful for this man with my voice. "Look," he said, addressing me informally, "there's a place on the corner where we can get a drink." We stopped. We got out. We ordered whiskey and coffee, that is to say, two whiskies and two coffees. The waiter seemed accustomed to receiving a set of twins who were, without him realizing it, always a different pair.

We drank. First, the coffee, which was very hot. Later, slowly, the alcohol. I stared at him intensely, especially when he didn't notice I was doing it. The following day I would be dressed the same, in a pale-blue jumpsuit and a pair of rubber-soled shoes. One of the university's rules was that no one be distinguishable by their clothing. Rings were forbidden. Haircuts were mandatory at the beginning of the month. In terms of academics, each fellow created his own curriculum. Or he didn't study at all. Or he read. Or wrote. Or played sports. Gonçalves, for example, having arrived at Lerna a few days earlier, was taking a course on electronics in the School of Mathematics.

During our chat, it came to my attention that the dormitories were situated around a circular corridor, onto which every door opened. The corridor encircled a grass-covered interior garden with a fountain, also circular, in the middle. The dormitories (in reality, they were apartments) were numbered. For now, Gonçalves was in apartment number twenty. I said we'd be seeing each other often. "Yes," he replied, "every day, but it won't be easy to recognize each other." I didn't reply to this observation. The only thing that occurred to me was a somewhat silly question. Was there a rapport between the fellows? "Of course there is, man," said the Portuguese. "We're not savages."

We left the bar and got back in the car, and ten minutes later we were going up the mountain by way of a torturous corniche. Lerna was a little more than twelve miles away. It was an old stone building, modernized on the inside and built on a tract of flattened land situated among four peaks of average height. The plain resulted from the convergence of four valleys and had the benefit of offering a country-like landscape rather than that of an oppressive mountainous region. Lerna sat at the highest altitude of any populated place in the area.

The building, dating from the end of the seventeenth century, was built by the French Benedictines, who had barely, or perhaps never, inhabited it. Lerna's theological investigations had begun obscurely, but it was definitively established as a school of theology under the protection of a group of wealthy nobles who preferred anonymity, perhaps due to the heterodox nature of their research. It was said that, in exchange for Lerna, one noble had given the order a property in the south of France.

In addition to the ring of twenty-four apartments, the monks built several wings that split off from the circle. In Lerna there were usually some two hundred students—or novices, as they were occasionally called, probably due to the university's origin—staying in the wings or pavilions. But every five years, the university went into recess for a year and the students abandoned the premises while the majority of the professors traveled to other centers of study. Only a few teachers remained at Lerna and continued their research linked to the old House: theology, mathematics, and law. This was a recess year and the university had invited twenty-four professionals from different parts of the world. The twenty-four of us were physically identical.

We entered via a gravel road lined with enormous trees. There were remnants of a recent snowfall. The path led to a grand building of irregular ashlars covered here and there by ivy that had been defeated by the cold. We left the car and crossed the threshold of an enormous hall. An extremely dignified-looking old man dressed in an impeccable tailcoat conducted us to the rector's office. He appeared to be mute.

Before I went in, Gonçalves said goodbye. "We'll see each other later, I hope," I said. "Yes, of course, I hope so too," he replied in a somewhat melancholy voice.

The rector wasn't so humble anymore. He seemed cold and distant. He greeted me and handed me a folder in which, he said, I would find the rules and layout of the university, a list of courses, an explanation of the mechanisms for communicating with professors, a schedule, and all of the other information necessary for living in Lerna. "Today is December 8. On June 8, I will see you at the same time to say goodbye, that is, if you haven't decided to leave before that." Ignoring my protests, he got up and, walking slowly and deliberately, accompanied me to the door. His office was really a luxuriously furnished library where, despite the large lit fireplace, there floated a delicious perfume of wood and tobacco.

Upon leaving the office I was once again received by the old man in the tailcoat. He wasn't mute; he told me that I would find my suitcase in room number twenty-four. He accompanied me to the circular hall and said goodbye with a tilt of his head.

Judging by the distance that separated one door from the other, I guessed that each fellow had his own large apartment. The circle of the hall or gallery was no less than ninety yards in diameter, and it did indeed surround an interior garden with a marble fountain in the center. The fountain resembled a sort of giant pineapple which shot thin streams of water. I was passing apartment twenty-two when I saw one of the fellows leave wearing his pale-blue jumpsuit. I couldn't contain myself and yelled, "Gonçalves!" The man came up to me and said his name was Jacques Dournier, he was studying theology, and he was Belgian. He was identical to me, that is to say, to Gonçalves. Dournier wished me luck and left, and I walked to my room ill-disposed to say hello to anyone no matter how similar to me, Dournier, or Gonçalves they might be.

The door to my apartment opened into a spacious foyer. I turned on the light and closed the numbered door behind me. In addition to the foyer, I had at my disposal a magnificent bedroom, a large bathroom, a study with a fireplace, and large windows that opened onto the opposite side of the circular hall. The furniture was solid and dark, the floors carpeted, and next to the desk, there was a large console with a record player, tape recorder, telephone, speakers, and radio. I opened the heavy curtains. From the window I could make out the deep and wooded night blending into a starless sky.

A brief note lay on the table. "We request that Doctor Beltra change before leaving his room. He will find his clothing in the dresser. Administrative Secretary (365)." I undressed and went into the bathroom. The abundant and heavy shower seemed to revive me from an old, almost forgotten death.

I put on the pale-blue jumpsuit. Looking at myself in the mirror, I couldn't help but think of Gonçalves and Dournier. Wearing unusual clothing is alienating, but this jumpsuit also evoked the two people I had seen wearing it. I thought about how, in a way, having the same face as other people was a means of disappearing from the world. A uniform equalizes and at the same time depersonalizes. But when a group wears the same uniform and its members are also physically identical, more than just equal and depersonalized, individuals are almost invisible. I strolled over to the telephone and dialed 365. A man answered. "Is it absolutely necessary that I put on this onesie?" I asked with obvious impertinence. "Yes," he said. Since I had expected some type of explanation, I ceased this line of questioning to hide my impotence and added, "I wanted to know where the dining hall is." Unruffled, like a machine, the man told me that "between rooms eight and nine you will find the door corresponding to wing D. To the right about twenty yards from the entrance, you'll find the dining hall. There's a detailed map of the entire university in your folder." I hung up without thanking him. If they were going to be curt with me, I hoped they would remember that I was a porteño, a specialist in maintaining my distance, and what's more, completely devoid of faith in that thing people call warmth.

I left my apartment and, after passing room number eight, found an enormous door identical to the one between my room and room number one, and to the door between rooms number four and five. I entered wing D and about twenty yards away found the dining hall.

Inside there were about twelve or fourteen circular tables made of mahogany. The light was rather weak but pleasant. The outfits everyone was wearing (pale-blue jumpsuits, exclusively) clashed violently with the severe luxury of the great dining hall: there were huge curtains over the large windows, walls covered in tapestries, large carpets, a wooden coffered ceiling richly painted in muted colors that repeated Lerna's predominant shape: the circle, but in this case, each one of the circles was inscribed in a square. Nevertheless, thanks to the effects of the paint, you could see in the ceiling a larger circle which was in turn inscribed around the perimeter of the dining hall. But what gave the impression (and certainty) of luxury was the polished silverware, the dishes, the sonorous and sparkling crystal wine glasses. Unaccustomed to such extreme and uniform quality, I had to make an effort to hide how intimidated I was by this refinement.

A few of the tables were empty. At others, two or three fellows ate and conversed. Very few were eating alone. I, of course, sat by myself, read the menu, and ordered a rice with curry that I had smelled when I first walked in. To accompany it, I ordered a French wine I had never tried before: Château Sérignac. I promised myself I would pay close attention to the labels, try all the bottles, and affiliate myself with the red I liked best. The waiter also gave off the impression he was mute. I felt true pity for myself when I realized none of the waiters at Lerna would know that Buenos Aires's rival soccer teams, Racing and Boca, even existed.

But the serious matter at hand wasn't Boca or the dining hall furniture or the French wine or the repeating circles. It was the fellows. There must have been about twenty of them, but it seemed like a million. They were not so much speaking as whispering (I think the atmosphere imposed it), and all in a very similar voice. The majority spoke to one another in French, and the only thing that prevented this from becoming a horrible torment were the two or three exceptions, which broke the uniformity: a conversation in German and another, in the distance, perhaps in Russian.

It was as if we were a single person reflected fully in each fragment of a shattered mirror. I imagined we all formed part of a single being captured in each moment of a grotesque contortion. I thought of another mirror, mobile and perverse, that with arbitrary skill would suddenly reproduce the many profiles of a man, invent for him innumerable hands, or give a simultaneous version of his face as it passed through pain and fear, stupor and happiness, love and hate, delirium and mockery.

I wondered what kind of evil mind would invent a reality capable of bringing the bravest man to the brink of insanity. This was undoubtably a trap, just as I had foreseen (although vaguely) while completing my paperwork.

I am a fairly shy person. But here I assumed that I would be protected by the anonymity that would inevitably come with being identical to the other fellows. Therefore, I figured I could join the other five fellows who were talking at the table farthest away from mine without any problem. I ordered a Hoyo de Monterrey cigar and, encouraged by my naive assumptions and the magic of the Château Sérignac, resolved to join the group. "Good evening," I said without removing the Havana from my mouth (I was using both hands to drag over a heavy chair). They greeted me and moved around to make room. Finding myself with people who were so similar to me gave me a great deal of confidence. "Whatever mistake I make," I said to myself, "will be understood and forgiven by these halfwits because, among other reasons, even our mistakes must be similar."

One of the fellows caught me up. "We were talking about Chartres." I acknowledged this with a slight nod to signal that the chat could proceed. Someone said something about the rib vaults: that the way they were resolved was totally (he looked for the precise adjective and pronounced it with emphasis, but I didn't hear him because I was too concentrated on his mannerisms, which in a way terrified me).

"That marvelous work," I said without being able to stop myself, as though the thought hadn't originated with me, but rather the Sérignac, "That marvelous work was only possible due to the existence of a group of people like ours, rigorously equal to ours." My observation created an abrupt and total silence. Finally, one of them asked me in a very neutral tone what I meant by a group "rigorously equal to ours."

"What I mean is 'depersonalized,' a group of anonymous people who are deindividualized, an organized human force, a group in which no one has been able to stand out." After a brief pause, another voice, from another guy (the voice sounded like mine and the guy seemed to be me), replied, addressing himself to the group. "That would make sense if Chartres was nothing more than a coherent work, but it also happens to be genius." There was another silence, this one more prolonged. "These people are contemptible," I thought. "And they'll be able to recognize me if I keep talking. They're clever and they must have a way of knowing who just got here. Maybe, for example, I shouldn't have said 'good evening' when I came over. A word denotes a style; an out-of-place comment is enough to give me away as a foreigner, which is what I am among these people."

"A human being, and only a human being, could create Chartres. Any accessory to it could have the utmost excellence, and even the utmost coherence with respect to the basic idea, but it would still be nothing more than an accessory," said another fellow with conviction.

I did not answer and nor did I feel like doing so. I could have just as easily made that comment myself and defended it until the end of time. A guy to my left, without taking the Havana out of his mouth and looking at the ceiling through the smoke, remarked, "Undoubtedly. Who can think of creation in terms of teams?" The waiter came over and offered coffee.

"Cognac," said one of the fellows. "For everyone," I added, forgetting that my criollo generosity would be useless here, since we were all guests. The five fellows looked at me without saying a word. "What's your name?" the one across from me finally asked. "Beltra," I answered, with a resignation that came from the depths of my soul. But I wasn't going to let them twist my arm, so I hid my surprise at having been discovered. "I'm from Argentina. I'm a lawyer. I arrived today." They shook my hand but none of them introduced themselves. I nearly showed weakness by asking them who they were, where they were from, but my pride kept me quiet. One of them, who had been silent the entire time, and without wiping a superior sort of smile off his face that wasn't at all foreign to me, said, "I know you." "Gonçalves!" I exclaimed with happiness. "No," he answered. "Dournier."

I drank the cognac and retired to my apartment.

A human body, tired to the point of exhaustion but well-fed, and with a perhaps excessive dose of alcohol, will climb between linen sheets and notice that, despite all its infamies, humanity has had the generosity to create a few small things that are almost sacred. I turned off the light and thought of

Sandra. Tucked into my memory of her as if in a distant, aquatic music, I fell asleep and slept like a log.

I woke up at eight o'clock in the morning. After a quick shower, I shaved and went to the dining hall. I devoured my breakfast with the hunger of a wolf. Luckily, there were packs of cigarettes on the table, which saved me the trouble of having to obtain them myself. From the dining hall, one passed through a reading room, and from there to the park, which was surrounded by forest. "It's time to reconnoiter the area," I thought, using military terms. It was very cold, but the pale-blue jumpsuit was miraculous. Next to a fireplace or exposed to the elements, one felt equally comfortable. That double woolen fabric had, without a doubt, some insulating material in the middle. It was bright out and the vestiges of snow were dissolving into vestiges of water that traveled down the tree trunks like translucent worms stretching to reach the earth. I walked alongside wing D observing its magnificent wall of gray ashlar, identical to the ones all surrounding the building. When I arrived at the end of the pavilion there was a stable. Seeing my interest, a man dressed in leather asked me if I was going for a ride. I said yes. Each wing or pavilion was no less than two hundred yards long and the idea of walking around the university was not very tempting.

I was given a chestnut and mounted it thinking of my years in the military and of Sergeant Soria, who handled the reins and horse blankets with the same skill as an intellectual does their books. "Gringos!" he would yell at us every time we messed up. I decided to ride out to the forest, the edge of which was very precise. A very lightly treed park surrounded the extensions, which shot out like spokes from the circular passage. There was nothing besides perfectly maintained lawn and isolated groups of small plants. Narrow gravel paths led to the end of the park, which was also circular. At the edge, dense vegetation started to slope slightly up toward the four valleys and four surrounding mountains.

I figured that if there were twenty-four apartments, and there was a wing every four entrances, there would be six wings in total. The forest closed in on my right, and to my left was the tract of flattened land with the enormous building. The path I was taking constituted Lerna's outer circle, with the fountain, the circular passage, the pavilions, and the park in its center. I estimated its circumference to be almost two miles.

Since all the rooms were identical, I thought it would be advisable to count them as I passed so as not to get lost when I returned. Later I realized this was a useless precaution: I could take a wrong turn, but the horse would not. I felt very Argentine riding that first morning in Lerna. I regretted not having visited Bariloche so I could confirm the superiority of our landscape, which of course goes without saying. That being said, I didn't deny the majesty of my surroundings: the trees in their beauty swayed slightly as the air circulated, thin and crystalline. In the afternoon, after lunch, I would dedicate myself to reviewing the contents of the folder they had given me and maybe take a short nap. The ride was stimulating. An hour of daily horseback riding, reading, talking with the other fellows, eating well, and drinking even better seemed like a good plan for the six months I had ahead of me. I would look into the law courses they offered, trying, of course, to reconcile what might be useful with that which wouldn't require too much effort.

I rode my horse al tranco, in the Argentine tradition. One should never forget that the Spanish word for chestnut is "zaino," which is also slang for false, and I didn't want to give the impression that Argentines aren't good horsemen. I saw from far away the recurring pavilions that opened like rays of a stone sun beneath the immense sky. I thought it would be very nice to see that strange solitary construction buried in the middle of four vegetation-covered peaks from a plane, with Sandra. I listened attentively to the squeak of the saddle beneath the weight of my body as though it were a music evoking the plains.

I decided to dismount and walk through the forest. I would leave the horse tied to a tree. I got off, crossed the stirrups at the height of the seat handle (just like I did in the military), and entered via a natural path that opened between large blue trees. The solitary calm was interrupted when, a few yards in, I bumped into a pair of fellows who were, of course, bundled up in their pale-blue jumpsuits and reading by the foot of a tree. I went up to them and introduced myself. Very affably, without telling me their names, they informed me that in Lerna it was not customary to introduce oneself. They added, as if flaunting a magical wisdom, that although they hadn't read my name on the bulletin board, there was no doubt I was the lawyer who'd arrived the day before from Argentina. I apologized for being ignorant of the local customs. I told them I practiced those that were considered good manners in my own country. Then, since I noticed that my reply and especially my tone betrayed a certain aggressiveness, I assured them that the night before, in the dining hall, a fellow in the group I had met seemed to have no problem asking me my name. "You must have broken a rule," one of them observed. Without seeing the connection between my story and his response, I assured them that that couldn't have been the case. "I was very courteous. I even offered everyone cognac." A different fellow hastened to add that that was the transgression; in Lerna, you could drink and smoke as much as you liked, but they asked that nobody offer alcohol or tobacco to anyone else. I processed this information but couldn't help saying that, despite being a lawyer, I felt a frank repulsion for any rule I didn't impose upon myself. I added that, although we suffered the inconveniences of frequent military revolutions and underdevelopment, in general in our countries everyone did what they felt like. I was a bit rude, and before bidding them goodbye, I highlighted my disdain for rules by offering them cigarettes. They didn't accept but explained it was only because they didn't smoke. "There's no rule against accepting," they said, "Just offering." "Coherence be damned!" I said, and then told myself that Protestants are all the same. I left them and returned to my chestnut.

On the ride back, I regretted not having agreed upon some sort of signal with Gonçalves so we would recognize each other. I was only interested in having a friend with whom I could speak freely, without thinking of rules. Maybe my only recourse was to phone him and invite him to my apartment. I left the horse after giving it a few pats and loosening the girth so the man dressed in leather would see that I knew my stuff.

I arrived at the entrance to the dining hall, staying on the path I knew until I got a feel for the place. I didn't want to get lost like a rat in this maze, which was complex despite its seeming simplicity. I walked through the dining hall toward the circular passage and from there to my apartment.

I picked up the phone and asked the operator to connect me with room number twenty. "Gonçalves?" I asked. "Yes," he answered without hiding his surprise. "Hey, man, it's me, Beltra, I wanted to see you for a second." After a silence that lasted far too long, I heard the Portuguese decline: he had a seminar later and still had a lot of reading to do. I hung up with evident displeasure. After all, I had just arrived, and thought I deserved special treatment according to the most basic rules of hospitality. I flung myself into the armchair in my study. Even among twenty-four men my own age, and with so many other similarities, I felt alone, as if I were living in an empty world. ("If only they'd awarded me a fellowship with Sandra!" I thought. But I was so upset that not even my own sense of humor could cheer me up.)

I left the apartment for lunch, hoping I wouldn't cross paths with any of the other fellows. There was a single empty table in the corner of the dining hall, and I rushed toward it. I counted how many of us there were. Twenty-four. Gonçalves must have been one of the two talking passionately about transistors and valves. I ate without looking up from my plate. That my own face and my own gestures were being used by twenty-three people seemed like an abominable repetition. There was no doubt about it: they were using us as guinea pigs. And we, surrounded by luxury and attended to like kings, let them do it, like people who sell their own blood. I was the last person to arrive at the dining hall and, of course, the first to leave.

On my way out, I lit my cigar and couldn't suppress a rude comment. "Fucking gringos!" I muttered and went to go read the rules.

I have transcribed from memory the most important ones as I remember them (they frequently used the word "novice" instead of "fellow").

—Avoid introductions when meeting with two or more fellows.

—Avoid pre-established signals or gestures for the purposes of recognizing one another.

—No one was allowed to tell anyone their apartment number. The only exception to this, as with the rule regarding introductions, was in cases where a new arrival's first encounters with the other fellows had clearly upset him.

—No one was allowed to turn down a request by the Administrative Secretary to go and receive a new fellow at the train station in Umsk.

—The guests would be forced to change apartments as many times as the rectory deemed appropriate. In those cases, there would be no reason to worry about one's personal items, or those taken on loan from Lerna's library, record collection, or art collection.

—Since the pieces in the art collection were of inestimable value, the paintings hanging in the apartments could not be moved. The gallery officials had considered the deterioration that the sun or heat might produce when they placed them. No one was allowed to borrow more than one painting at a time nor would a painting be loaned for more than three weeks. Exchanges could be made through Lerna's curator, who, in the event that he did not receive any requests, would move the works according to his personal criteria.

—It was expressly forbidden for fellows to visit each other in their apartments.

—Asking a novice's name was permissible only when he was clearly breaking a rule.

—They asked that nobody offer alcohol or tobacco to a fellow guest. However, there would be tobacco and alcohol available for whomever wanted it.

—Haircuts were mandatory within the first three weekdays of every month.

—The university's objective in gathering a group of individuals with identical physical characteristics was kept completely secret. Everyone was allowed to consider, judge, assess, and interpret the fact in any way they pleased, but the university reserved the right not to communicate the objective of the "project" to any individual fellow or group.

—Lerna had posted specialists in different parts of the world to find candidates, which is how they had established our whereabouts.

—All languages were permitted, but they recommended the use of French, which everyone in the group spoke.

—If, for whatever reason, a fellow wanted to rescind the contract and leave the university before the date established by the fellowship, they needed to leave a letter addressed to the rector in the mailbox across the door from wing B. This letter had to be delivered at least seven days in advance of when the fellow wanted to leave so the authorities could obtain and coordinate the tickets to Geneva and to the country of origin of the interested party.

—Lerna recognized that the novices' presence was an honor for the university and so they were deeply appreciative of the sacrifice that temporarily abandoning one's country, daily tasks, friends, and family required, to the benefit of the science in which each was going to specialize.

—In exchange, the university offered the opportunity to deepen one's knowledge in one of the schools' three disciplines: theology, mathematics, and law.

—Lerna felt obligated to inform the fellows that in the interest of the work they were doing—that is, the "project"—they would be taking the liberty of filming a group or individual fellows for up to five hours per day while they went about their different activities. The filming could occur at any time and without prior notice. They would likewise be recording conversations or lectures in the dining hall or the classrooms, on car rides, in the libraries, or in the reading rooms. The recording would occur ten hours per week and without prior notice. They informed us that under no circumstance would a fellow be recorded or filmed in his apartment, during moments which were considered inviolably private. They guaranteed the university would never attempt to identity those who were filmed and whose words they were recording, and they would only use those testimonials as material for their "project." When someone in a recording or film revealed his name, the material would be immediately destroyed.

—The novices were informed that there were microphones in many different places and cameras that covered practically the entire building, even Lerna's gardens. They reiterated, however, that inside their apartments, their guests would be guaranteed the utmost privacy.

I'm positive my own reaction to the rules mirrored that of the other fellows: an immediate feeling of offense, followed by a total lack of interest in the "project."

Very rarely did we allude to or speak directly of the matter. The rules of the game were clear, and I don't think anybody felt very affected by the possible consequences of what some began to call "the research." Nobody liked being filmed or having their conversations recorded, especially during moments when they were unaware of or not expecting it, but a general lack of interest in the "project" allowed us to proceed with the greatest freedom and naturalness. They weren't recording us doing anything truly private, and considering the certainty that nobody was saying or doing anything that should be hidden, the possible films or recordings were not very interesting. Nobody could record our desires, our unexpressed thoughts, only our behavior with one another or in a group.

I will not hide the fact that, personally, I felt a sort of "scientific respect" for all this, and although it did not awaken my solidarity with the rules and the "project" itself, it contributed to the erasure of my initial reaction.

In any event, whether for lack of interest or their own sense of comfort, nobody was much bothered by "the investigation" and everybody spoke and worked with total spontaneity, perhaps due to the certainty that it was impossible to be identified.

Under careful observation, each fellow had some subtle characteristic that made him unique. Particular ideas or
words, ways of looking, inflections, how he paid attention,
attack and defense mechanisms, unformulated opinions hidden in a gesture, and, on top of all this, the one thousand resources of a face, of its muscles, of the voice and its silences.
Ultimately, everyone speaks a unique language, and even
though everyone spoke in the same tongue, it wasn't too
difficult, if one set out to do it, to tell people apart. Naturally, our individual styles were hidden behind our similar
exteriors, by the similarities of our voices, and—as I at one
point suspected—by the ongoing imitations of styles foreign
to our own. Perhaps, and this was most likely, everyone
was just continuing to be as unique and individual as they
could despite the similarity and constant depersonalization
to which we were submitted. But sometimes, repeating the
mannerisms of the person in front of you was inevitable,
and even a way to confirm the equality that, on one level,
we had rejected but that, on another, we had to reaffirm,
because it was the starting point of everyone's individuality.
If for us the individualization of a fellow was practically impossible, there was no doubt that for the people in charge of
the "project" it had to be even more difficult.

One afternoon, in the bar next to the covered swimming pool,
I began chatting with one of the fellows. He told me he was
interested in literature, and while I don't think crime novels
were his specialty, he had envisioned almost every feasible way
a murder could occur inside a community like ours without it
being possible to identify the criminal. It was a long conversa-

tion in which at times I contributed ideas, as though I were an accomplice to the terrible fantasies that passed through his mind. Our voices echoed on the water underneath the glass roof and our words resonated and became prolonged. At one point, I got our words so mixed up that I didn't know which one of us had said them. Hearing the horrors he elaborated in a voice at once identical and foreign to mine was terrifying. "If there were a string of murders in the group, and supposing I were the murderer, finally two of us would remain. In that case, I should let myself be killed by the other so the survivor would be charged guilty and executed."

I think he was the most tortured guy at Lerna. Perhaps the negatives of the sinister game we were involved in were clearer to him. We were drinking vodka, and I asked him if he frequently had conversations like this. He said no. He remembered only one similar one, with a novice he had gone to pick up in Umsk and with whom he had spent six hours drinking in town: "The other guy was an Irish novelist," he said. "I'm a hopeless drunk." We dived into the water. There were a couple of fellows swimming in the pool. I never knew if I spoke to him again.

At Lerna, life was not just a limp succession of weeks where nothing happened. Whatever one did not say or do was done or said by the others. I protected my solitude. Instinctively, I knew—and I was sure I wasn't mistaken—that the more time I spent alone, the better I would feel. I listened to lots of music, read for many hours, and didn't sleep for even a minute less than is humanly possible. I signed up for a class with a Professor Conradd, a Polish jurist with whom we worked in the library of wing F. At the beginning, there were three of us students, but within a few weeks I was the only one who remained loyal to his classes, which consisted of lectures and textual commentary. A paragraph from one book led us to another book and after two hours of work we were submerged in a great number of volumes that had followed from the old man's train of thought.

I learned to be alone. I learned that the good thing about solitude is that it reinforces our certainty of being alive (something that was very necessary at Lerna). Every moment could be full and beautiful. It was enough to look at the arrises on the ceiling or get a whiff of tobacco, to enjoy the fragrant air of the forest, or ride my horse in order to live the good life. And so, my life began to resemble my most intimate thoughts and passions.

Eventually I tamed the chestnut. I have evidence that he became noble, that I made him brave (made him a pingo, as we'd say in Argentina) and erased the zaino in him forever. Unless it was raining or snowing, I always took him for a ride. And even when it did rain or snow, I would go to the stable to pet him and bring him a sugar cube. Perhaps there were better horses at Lerna; I don't know. But I thought that I had been given this chestnut, this zaino, like someone is given a destiny.

I don't usually talk about what's private, but from what I've already said, it's easy to imagine that behind my hours and days, the image of Sandra was always there. "The Argentine woman . . ." I said to myself, as if I were acquainted with every skirt on the planet. Sure, it's true that I didn't complete the sentence, but that was unnecessary. I thought about her voice, tried to recapture her face, clearing away interferences in my memory that denied me it, and when I found it, I contemplated it for a moment, and then rejected it with a resigned wisdom. After all, it wasn't worth going crazy over. With her I would walk the streets of Buenos Aires. Unless her flights, her visits to other countries, her comings and goings, had erased me from her memory? I thought that to think about her was to retain her. That saving her a place in my future was looking after her present. And so, that's how it was, I studied, I read, I drank, I had a horse, and I thought about Sandra.

The dining hall was the only place in Lerna where all of the fellows got together at the same time. Frequently I counted them, and almost always at one in the afternoon and nine thirty at night there were twenty-four of us. Very infrequently, one or two were missing.

Halfway through March I noticed a slight decrease in the number of fellows. I think only a few people needed to go missing for their absence to be conspicuous. I dare say even the activity of the waiters had diminished, and the murmur of the conversations wasn't the same as before. As small as these changes to the dining hall were, they were notable because, in a way, the time we spent there was the most pleasant: it gave us the chance to talk, have fun, and frequently, hear about things that were truly interesting.

When I finally worked up the courage to share my suspicion that there were fewer of us, I received the unpleasant confirmation that my impression was widely shared. Before several meals, I took pains to arrive very early, and I would delay my exit as long as possible to avoid errors in my calculations. And yet, we were never more than twenty.

I shared my observations with another group, and everyone was clearly worried. At this point I wasn't the only one keeping track of who was missing. The anxiety became generalized, and it soon became the inevitable topic of conversation.

The rules at Lerna required the publication, via the classroom bulletin boards, of everyone's comings and goings. We fellows had been joined together within fifteen days of each other, and when I, the last, had arrived, the list of twenty-four guests was complete. There had been no desertions announced, and therefore, it was supposed that everyone continued to complete the six-month period as stipulated in the contract. The absences, then, had no justification, and some believed they were a reasonable cause for alarm.

No one had any idea what was behind this mystery. But, for the first time, I think, an uneasiness blossomed that connected (albeit imprecisely) the disappearance of fellows with Lerna's secret project. The only thing that was certain was that no one had left the university and there were no longer twenty-four of us.

By the end of March, the number of people in the dining hall had continued to thin. The absences had markedly increased over the last few days. There were four of us at my table, and one of the fellows—no doubt to delay the pressing issue concerning us—began to explain a very serious problem having to do with soccer in his country. I thought he might be Uruguayan, but it turned out he was English. I was savoring my Sérignac when the rector appeared. It was the first time I had seen him since the day of my arrival, and I don't think the others had seen him either. We stood up and listened to the news. "Gentlemen," he said, "I am sorry to inconvenience you, but I am obliged to do so due to the gravity of the situation." Our surprise at seeing the old man quickly turned to alarm. His words smelled of disaster. "I take it for granted," he added, "that I can count on the greatest calm on your part in these circumstances. One of the fellows has just died and there are seven who are severely ill. The nature of this sudden epidemic has bewildered the doctors."

Upon word of the outbreak, the national authorities had hastened to impose a quarantine. No one could leave Lerna for the next six weeks. The date would be moved if new cases occurred. Umsk did not have adequate facilities to intern the sick, but doctors and equipment were arriving from there and Geneva.

A fellow asked the rector for the names of those dead and sick. "We all know from the bulletin boards the names of the fellows who entered. We all had a special bond with the one who picked us up in Umsk (except for the first fellow to arrive, who surely met the second). I don't know how important it is to know who has died or who is sick," he clarified, "but I'm asking offhand." The rector interrupted him harshly. His words were so disdainful, so distant from the mellifluous tone of his letters. He claimed knowing the names meant nothing. That there was no such thing as friendship among the fellows. That knowing the names didn't matter. "It does matter," cut in another, speaking forcefully. "And I think it's unnecessary for you to understand why. But I know it's important to all of us." Annoyed, the rector explained categorically that it should be enough to know that he wasn't the dead man. "I'm not sure it's not me!" shouted the fellow.

Unanimously, we demanded the right to know the names. With evident displeasure, the old man declared, "Dr. Dournier is dead." The news shocked me greatly, as if his death were more important than any other. "Dr. Serella and Dr. Morgan, the architects Salin and Loudez, the engineer Gonçalves, the novelist O'Hara, and the priest Bermúdez are ill." Gonçalves as well? According to the rector, their condition was extremely dire, and from now on he would keep us informed about what was going on. As he left, he seemed more upset about having to tell us the names than the tragedy devastating the university.

The next day only fifteen of us ate lunch together. Although the sensible thing to do was stay apart to avoid the possibility of contagion, the truth is we were spending more time with each other than ever. We put three tables together and it was obvious we were all trying not to panic. We—all of us—discussed communicating with the rectory to attend Dournier's funeral service. Our request was denied. What we really wanted to know was whether the fellow who had been missing since the night before was also sick. Someone asked for cognac. When the waiter arrived, the one whose idea it was to drink asked if he could use the phone to call the rectory. When they had them on the line, the fellow went to speak and, upon his return, announced: "In his typically indirect style, the rector has informed me that we are the only novices unaffected by the epidemic."

The trap was closing. We were doomed to an irremediable death. The violence of the disease would drag every one of us down. One of the fellows excused himself hastily and left the dining hall. I examined his neck, his hands, his back, his feverish face, which for an instant turned around to look at me. A slight tremor roamed his body. I was certain that, in the subtlest way he could, he would walk with a secret dignity toward his death. He chose decorum from all the possible recourses. I stirred with pride as if he were my brother.

"Another cognac," I ordered. When the waiter approached, I offered it to everyone, and everyone accepted. "And bring us some cigars," I added. Almost everyone smoked. Without looking at anyone, I raised my voice to say, "In case they are filming or recording, let it be known that I am Beltra, the same that just offered cognac and tobacco." And I told myself that if I had to die, I would do it without complying with these absurd rules.

A few seminars began at three in the afternoon. I understood the group's dispersal to be an innocent attempt at prolonging a normality that certainly no longer existed. We said goodbye until lunchtime. ("That is, if there's nothing better to do," said one of the fellows with a questionable sense of humor.)

I was living in room number three, which had a painting I didn't care for. I put on a record I had been listening to a lot. The lover sang of his wish to be left alone to die. The five voices, the five times the five singers sang the line, were all unified in a single protagonist who from tenor passed to soprano, from alto to baritone, then to another tenor, and finally to the individualized group. It was as if they were different layers of the same being, representing all human possibilities, and ending up integrated into a solitary lament. With unbridled romanticism, I devoted myself to thinking of Sandra. The music and lyrics were certainly not festive or appropriate to the circumstances, but their great beauty was irrefutable. The silence was harsh when the record player stopped. Inside that chamber, I felt as though I were already dead. "Somehow," I told myself, "those who die in this story will die in me. They have something of my own life in them."

I slept until five o'clock. Before dinner I had class with Conradd, and I thought not attending would cause him pain. I had gained his esteem and my absence would inevitably alarm him. I went to class, and we worked together for a long time.

Lunches and dinners had become sinister meetings that marked the progress of death. Every day there were fewer of us, and everyone seemed to be deteriorating physically, perhaps because of the disease. Or maybe it was our fear that consumed us as efficiently as any virus.

Early one morning I heard footsteps and voices in the circular hallway. I jumped out of bed and peered into the dark corridor. A few nurses or doctors wearing masks and ghostly white uniforms removed a stretcher from the apartment adjacent to mine. With a frantic gesture, I was instructed to close my door. On the stretcher, I saw a body covered with a sheet. Two other men, also dressed in white, entered the apartment with a large aerosol container, without a doubt to disinfect it. I went back to bed. That dead body was identical to mine, and I was unable to stay my uncontrollable and unhealthy imagination. I pictured my own face turned cyanotic, blood-less, stiff with death. I remembered the fellow shouting that he wasn't sure he wasn't the dead man whose name they'd want-ed to hide from us. I remembered that when I turned to look at him, I found many faces identical to mine. I remembered that whoever had shouted had done it with my own voice.

And once again, it was Sandra who tore me away from that demonic whirlwind. I thought, "I don't want to die far away from her, without seeing her again. I don't want to be far away from my city, a city entirely mine to love and dis-cover with her." It hardly matters where death finds you, but that didn't mean it wasn't irritatingly unfair that destiny was employing this strange mechanism to annihilate us with the harsh blindness of someone committing a genocide. One by one, our kind was falling as if a curse was upon us. Formulat-ing it thusly was like peeking at a tragic and execrable truth. Why this curse? What were we most guilty of? I had spoken, presumably, with each of the fellows, and if there was any-thing they had in common (aside from their physical likeness), it was a transparent decency, an invariable interest in their neighbor, and even a poignant seriousness about their work. It was as if everyone, in understanding that they didn't receive the fellowship and its attendant privileges for any other reason than their random similarity, strived to become worthy of it. And then I felt the violence of anger and the fire of rage, and I regretted not being able to put up a fight against this injustice. I despised this death because I was being denied a battle.

From that day on, everything was dizzy and brutal. A cruel treachery infiltrated the air itself, and everything began to smell of venom and terror. I noticed it with disgust, but I disguised it for everyone else's sake. Everyone else probably noticed it, too, and like me, pretended to act naturally so as not to brew fear and rebellion.

Danger gathers people, brings them together, compels them to live with one another in order to face it. And so, we gathered, as if being separated made us more vulnerable. I confess I felt a great need for solitude. I preferred to wait for death alone, and yet I understood that the adult thing to do was not to indulge myself. I had a duty toward the others: to give them my presence.

One night, at dinnertime, the rector came down to visit us. He was altered, gray, and trembling when he announced that eight novices—this is what he usually called us—had died and that nine were sick. There were no comments. The seven of us that remained were silent. No one asked for the names. The disease was so merciless that even terror felt like a weak response to it.

I ordered my noble Sérignac and drank it as if it were the antidote to the grim poison that was invading our bodies. One of the fellows, a very sensitive and intelligent guy, started a conversation (I don't want to say about what). It let us spend a very sweet moment together. At last, we said our goodbyes. I didn't sense any anger. If everyone was afraid, we all kept it to ourselves, as if it were something personal and not transferable. That was the last night I ate with my classmates.

The following day I ate lunch alone. I had my class with Conradd at six o'clock. We read (he translated) an old Polish text about suicide. The rector didn't make an appearance at dinner. I finished eating and went to the park with my cigar. It was obvious: everyone else had fallen. It was an uneasy solitude. I was waiting my turn.

If my relationship with the fellows was, at first, defined by a mixture of benevolence and irony, I now understood that, in a mysterious and unconfessed way, I had learned to love them, to enjoy their outbursts of violence and humor, to see with indulgence their incipient erudition and admire the passion with which they defended their ideas. I could not help but feel true respect for the wholesome lack of regard with which they allowed themselves to be investigated, as if a clean and virile pride put them above Lerna's secret project. I knew full well that without the group's influence, and faithful to my own nature, I would not have been able to respond in such a carefree way to this kind of imposed mystery.

With sincere tenderness, I thought of those young men who were so similar to me that I often felt unable to distinguish between our behavior, between my voice and their voices. Those who were still alive, I knew, were dreaming their last dreams. Without a doubt, my turn to follow them would come up in the next few hours. There was an apparent plane where it was hard to make out the boundaries between the fellows and me, but it was also clear that I was a solitary person. Amid these digressions, I was a self that felt waves of terror and mortal fear. At times, I identified with the deceased and was hurt by their abandonment and the absences they created. But by the time I finished the cigar, I understood that I had to take great care with my own emotions. I didn't want to use sorrow for the dead as a disguise for unpardonable self-pity. Perhaps—most likely—I was already infected. That was a problem. The others were dead or dying. And that was another problem. I had the right to be terrified by the former, but pity was something I could only feel for the rest of them.

The rector didn't give me any news. I kept up my outings through the woods, my lonely meals, my Sérignac, and my cigars. What seemed at first to be a luxury had become a modest habit not too different from my routines in Buenos Aires, with my daily meals at the cheap restaurant on Venezuela Street. What I cared about most was Conradd's classes. I will leave out the nightmares, hopes, panics, and joys that I had or stopped having. None of it matters in this story. They had taken away the records I cared so much about and, according to the rules, I had to let a month pass before I could request them again. Conradd was my main interest, and on Saturdays I suffered our separation because it meant I wouldn't see him again till Monday. The only times I heard my own voice were when I was with him or when I ordered my meals.

One morning the phone in my apartment rang. It was the rector: it had been five weeks since the last death was recorded and I had to decide if I wanted to leave when the quarantine was lifted. It was not an invitation for me to leave, but according to the rules, in order to terminate the contract, I had to file my application that same morning.

I answered sharply that I still had seven days to get sick. And that I had also decided to stay until I had completed the term fixed by the fellowship, which was several weeks away. But, in exchange, I would ask for some exceptions to Lerna's rules: I would continue to meet with Conradd on Sundays, I'd be allowed to bring bottles of wine to my apartment, I wouldn't be moved from my apartment again, I wouldn't cut my hair anymore, they wouldn't force me to wear the jumpsuit, and I would be allowed to wear my civilian clothing. I would no longer let them film or record my classes, and I would be able to hold on to the Italian record I loved. And there would be no communication between me and the authorities at Lerna until the day of my departure. Finally, I asked that if I contracted the disease and died, they would communicate with my country's consul, for whom I would leave an envelope in my personal suitcase.

The rector assured me that at that very moment he would take the necessary measures to see to and authorize my requests. He said goodbye excitedly, thankfully, even blissfully. Mellifluous letters, contempt for other people's pain, humility, disdain, gratitude; every time I had contact with that strange character he showed a different face, as if all possible human forms were hidden inside of him.

I ended the conversation and left my apartment. Down the hall, in the dining hall and the park, behind the silences and the shadows, were voices echoing from the long pavilion. It was my own repeated voice that spoke of God and women, cathedrals and horses, politics and soccer, Cranach and Monteverdi, hell and the heavenly bodies.

I took advantage of Conradd's classes as much as I could. I listened to my favorite record over and over again. I brought many bottles of Sérignac to my apartment. I read for long hours in a state of peace I had never known before. Every morning I circled the university with my zaino. At dusk, I walked through the woods. The ghostly pale-blue figures had vanished forever. Perhaps I had only perceived them with my heart.

On the day of my departure, I packed my suitcase and put on the record player. I left my door open and, for the last time, as I walked down the circular hall, heard the single and solitary lover with five different voices, begging to be allowed to die.

I waited a few minutes in his office for the rector to arrive. He had aged so much or perhaps become so spiritualized that he no longer looked like himself. Purely out of routine and not because he was interested, he asked me how I would travel to Umsk. If it was possible, I said, I'd go on my horse. The train was leaving at dawn, and I had time to spare. I asked if someone could see to my suitcase and then bring the zaino back. He agreed. I said goodbye to the old man and went to the stable. I said hello to the man dressed in leather and turned the old horse toward the south.

I climbed the mountain at a gallop and, from there, looked at Lerna. It leaned against the hill under a beautiful moon that played hide-and-seek behind the wooded slopes, I went down alone, very alone, always al tranco, thinking about Sandra's eyes and whistling and singing, "Let me die."

In the immense, star-filled night, I heard my voice echo, multiplied by the hills. But I knew the voice was unique and mine and that with it, I would have to give my final answers.

STORIES

The Fire

I TOSSED THE MATCH and left without looking back. Before I'd reached the gate, I heard the hurricane-like sound erupt behind me. It was the sound of air exploding in a chain, bubble after bubble. Calmly, I crossed the atrium and locked the heavy iron door. I made my way to the square and took my time climbing the rubber tree in order to see the spectacle from up here, from this very branch. I had imagined it so many times before. The key in my pocket bothers me a little, but at the same time, it assures me of my power.

The night was empty. I alone seemed destined to witness the catastrophe. Strangely, though, just a few minutes after I'd settled on my branch, the square began to fill with people. As if they'd sprouted from the asphalt and sidewalks and grass, hundreds—maybe thousands—of people now contemplate my work. The first ones to notice the fire were driving a truck. All the traffic coming along the avenue behind them has stopped. Now there are lots of cars trapped by the people. Some of them have climbed on top of the cars to get a better view, leading to fights with the drivers, who are powerless before the arrogance of the crowd.

The lights went on in the nearby apartment buildings. It's like a party. All the balconies have chairs. So perhaps more like a theater. Many people have stayed where they are because you can see better from up high. I think it's mostly older people, but maybe I'm wrong, maybe it's the young who stay out to enjoy the view. I don't know. It looks like a political protest. Without a doubt now there are thousands of people. They cross themselves. Many cry. Many of them are grave and conspicuously silent. When the firemen arrived, they had to drive away a group of do-gooders trying to put out the flames with useless buckets of water.

When the firemen finally pried open the iron door with a crowbar, and later, knocked down the gate with a battering ram, you could see into the church. It was bright and shining like the inside of a boiler, like the muffle of a great furnace, like a forge. It was a single fiery mass. I had the key in my hand now. The streams of water shot from the atrium were lost in a blaze of yellow, red, and blue. It brought to mind a terrible fury, something definitive and horribly serene.

At first, a good part of the bell tower was covered in smoke. Then it was completely engulfed. They pulled out two asphyxiated friars and stuck them in an ambulance in vain. Below me I could hear some old ladies crying hysterically and shrieking:

"Father Jaime tried to get to the high altar to save the relics but was trapped by the flames."

The police try to get the crowd to clear out, but the crowd refuses to move.

I'm dying to smoke a cigarette. I'm going to light one up. If someone were to find me here, perhaps they'd think I'm just a spectator who's come for a better view. It's strange, but no one else has thought to climb the rubber tree, truly nature's greatest watchtower. Sitting on one of its wide branches, your weight causes it to give a little, lowering the leaves and allowing you the perfect view. It keeps you hidden, too, so you can watch and reflect free from the crowd below. I must say, the crowd behaves just like they do at mass: a few opaque murmurs here and there, except when something important happens, and then their voices spread like wildfire, and the old ladies below, for example, unleash their hysteria. In general, though, the silence is commendable.

More people arrive. About one hundred and fifty feet from the rubber tree, a group has gone down on their knees. Everywhere one goes, there's always someone who assumes the role of leader. It's almost always some bald guy with a deep voice—I can vaguely see him from here—who, inspired by the spontaneity of those who are even more religious than he is, orders, "Let us pray." Very few people pay attention to him. Eventually, as if by contagion, almost everyone is down on their knees. It's a marvelous spectacle. Now there must be about five or six thousand people kneeling at my feet. Meanwhile, I smoke and watch how the implacable tongues of fire, long and thin, voracious though unpredictable, climb toward the bell tower.

More firefighters arrive on the scene. I get the sense there are so many of them near the church that it's difficult for them to work. What's more, I'm positive what they're doing is useless. (They're professionals, so they must know this, too.) This won't stop until everything is reduced to ash. Suddenly it occurs to me that the bell is hanging from a thick wooden beam. When it burns up, the bell will come crashing down. Various collapses have already been heard. And yet! There are hundreds of gallons of gasoline intelligently distributed, strategically located. Every demijohn that explodes is like a new fire within the fire.

And to think Father Jaime was so grateful this morning for my dedication to the job! "It won't be long," he said, "until you'll have to replace our dear Paiva (the sacristan). He's getting old, just like I am, and we must make way for those who have followed us faithfully." But surely the faithful have been burnt up like rats, unless they've jumped over the wall to the homeless shelter or landed in the cemetery. I doubt a single friar has made it out alive, not to mention poor Paiva, who could barely move because of his rheumatism.

A gap opened up in the crowd and people started shouting. An enormous car moving at an ant's pace made its way through. My mind went blank as I tried to hear what was going on. Like they were on my payroll, the old ladies filled me in: the cardinal, the nuncio, and the mayor had arrived. There were rumors—still unconfirmed—that the president was on his way. If so, the police sirens would warn me.

But now that the officials were here, it seemed like we were ready for the denouement. "The bells!" they all cried at once. Their cries were clipped, like those of a great actor capable of shouting in a whisper. A low cry, but uniform. Even the people who were standing (probably in an act of defiance against that old man trying to put himself in charge of the fire), knelt down, and an incredible silence fell over the crowd. The fire, however, roared like a fighting animal, like an animal who knows the price of victory will be its own sacrifice.

The nuncio and the cardinal, followed by the mayor, cut a narrow path through the crowd and headed toward the church. There was something almost ritualistic about the way they walked through the crowd; they were the "adults," and the little bald man took advantage of this moment to break the silence and cry, "Lord, forgive us our sins . . . Have mercy . . . Have mercy . . ." And the crowd, as if it had rehearsed, repeated in a chorus, "Forgive us . . . Have mercy." His sobs grew louder as he repeated the plea three or four times, and the others' sobs grew louder, too. In the end, everyone was crying. The nuncio, the cardinal, and the mayor (the latter timidly and after some hesitation) crossed their arms until the dramatic pleas had ended. Everyone was crying and praying. And I was up here watching this incredible spectacle.

What I've done here is very important. I'm overcome with emotion, and wouldn't know how to explain this sort of happiness that's also mixed with tears. Swayed by the crowd, I began to pray, but luckily, I've come back to seeing things objectively.

You can tell they want to put out the fire from above, but even with all their fire trucks and ladders, it's clear to me they're destined to fail. Despite having put up a worthy fight, they've achieved absolutely nothing. It's as if they'd been spraying gasoline instead of water, because the fire rages stronger with every passing moment. The small-veined alabaster window panes have already fallen out. (The veining in the stone made them look like skin.) Now flames are coming out of the windows and devouring the walls. With incredible aim, the firemen manage to fill these apertures with their violent and useless jets of water. But as soon as they look for another target, flames leap out from where the light used to enter through the stone.

The sacristy was probably the first area to collapse. Hardly anyone knows that under the floor, to the left of the main nave, along with the tombs where the old friars are buried, there's an enormous storage area containing colonial paintings, icons, clothing, and furniture. There are also about forty small ebony and bronze boxes that hold the bones—surely dust now—of the convent's founders. The boxes are lined up on a shelf like a toy cemetery. That's where I put the gasoline. I was the only one who had the key to the padlock. For the last three months, I've been buying gasoline from different stations and bringing it down in demijohns. That cellar was basically a powder store. They say they discovered the door to it about twenty years ago (they're always finding new doors in old churches). As I doused the pews and altars, I took great pains so the gasoline would run down the stairs through the small door that leads to the chapel of San Pedro. Everything went according to plan. Every time the fire reached a new demijohn there was another explosion. It was as if gasoline had rained down on all the altars. And along the small corridor that surrounds the naves, at the height of the chapiters, I'd carefully placed demijohns where the beams met the walls.

By now, the newspaper and magazine photographers have already taken thousands of photos. A little while ago, one of them said, "I'm going to climb that tree," and I froze in place so he wouldn't see me. Luckily, a moment later, a massive collapse was heard. The fool ran toward the fire as if he could photograph the past and forgot all about the tree. The ceiling had caved in, and for an instant, it seemed to have squashed the flames. A moment later, though, protected by the exterior walls, the flames started climbing into the sky again, stronger than before. Then, as though tired of their work, the flames subsided. When the front of the church collapsed, the work was complete: everything was rubble.

A few ice cream vendors sat on the ground. Their boxes were empty. The nougat and waffle vendors, and the old man selling lollipops, had sat down, too. Nobody was selling anything anymore. The crowd had eaten everything. I lit another cigarette. My nose was dry, probably from the smoke. At that moment, the sun began to rise. Everyone was sitting on the ground. Very few people were still on their knees. Many of them cried, seemingly out of habit. I think there were more people now than there had been at night. In any case, from my branch, I could no longer see a single street that wasn't filled with the silent crowd. The fire trucks were empty. The firemen were sitting on the ground, too, staring at the inescapable landscape of ruins. There was complete silence. Nothing could be heard except the crackling rise of a dark column of smoke coming from the church site, which now seemed larger than when it was standing. I decided I would soon come down from the tree and walk like a God among the vanquished.

I looked in the direction of the authorities. The cardinal and the mayor were still sitting on the ground. The nuncio was standing. I sat and thought for a while. Those statues and icons I loved; how could they have crumbled under the violence of the fire? My good Saint Paul, with his glass eyes, that statue of the Virgin, identical to the one they worshipped in Andalusia, the wrought-iron railings, and the other saints, and the chandeliers, and the majolicas representing the seasons, the letters and the signs, and that noble golden paten embellished with piety. And the pulpit? It must have exploded like a nut bursting out of its shell. It reminded me of a floating tulip without its stem. I thought about the abat-voix, that useless but beautiful little roof. I used to look at the pulpit and think of it as a sort of flower, or a luxurious box of chocolates. Especially when Father Jaime (so skinny, wrinkled, and wormy) was giving the eleven o'clock sermon. The pulpit's abat-voix was like the lid of the box, and I thought that at any moment it would fall on Father Jaime and leave him trapped in mortal darkness. Often, when the church was empty, I would go up to the pulpit and stay still and silent for a long time, and let the dense serenity and unyielding calm of the place surround me. It was like being surrounded by death. And then the pulpit would turn back into a flower placed in the air, a golden flower suspended in the air as if by miracle. I put lots and lots of gasoline inside of it. I wanted the fire to be swift, intense, and definitive when it reached the pulpit, which I had cleaned so many times with loving dedication, and where I had spent so many moments playing at holiness.

What a sudden and surprising end for the church's usual stillness. The candles, melted before the fire even touched them, would have abandoned their tribute and fallen limp, as if life had been slit from their veins. In the tunnels below, there were cupboards full of lavender and starched linen, chasubles, and the purple cloths they used to cover the icons. Everything must have surrendered itself to the fiery holocaust with joyful submission, because the surprise must have added a new dimension to it all, and the purer the objects, the more likely they joined the celebration with certainty that it was all for the Glory of God. And in this way, they must have allowed themselves to become that which engulfed them: destruction and fire. At one point, I myself came to think that it would not be without grandeur to leap from this branch and run to the center of the fire, in a kind of personal sacrifice, for the simple and not inconsiderable beauty of offering my life to the spectacle. But I also thought that if I wanted to die for the church, I could just shout, "Here is the key used by the last person to leave the church." Then, convinced that would only cause confusion, I thought it better to shout: "I burned down my church!" I'd shout it in such a way that it would make everyone jump out of their seats, and free those wrathful penitents who usually keep their hatred coiled up like a spring, like a cat ready to pounce or an archer with his bow drawn. They're just waiting for me to confess so they can prove they're not wicked, that they're not the ones responsible for the fire, that I'm the guilty one. They wait on my confession so they can pounce and destroy me, annihilating me even more efficiently than the fire. But no. I am no suicide case. I feel . . . I know they know I'm here. As long as I don't reveal myself, they will continue to feel guilty. Each and every one of them feels responsible for the fire. Even though the fire is mine. No. I won't say it was me. Nor do I deserve the honor of such a sacrifice.

An ash-colored light rises from the river and my secret is sweet to me. I feel as if I've grown wings. A secret pair of wings that no one can see, but that I can use inside my heart.

It's all over now. I guess the crowd is willing to wait around these stinking ruins forever. Not me. The nuncio has his arms crossed again. Some people pray, others secretly talk among themselves. The streets and sidewalks are packed. Everyone has ended up sitting on the ground. Even the police. They all seem to be dreaming. It's very calm. It's the calm of empty hearts and broken wills. Of exhaustion, perhaps. Or maybe boredom. Now everything is finished. Carefully, I make my way to the trunk of the rubber tree and slide down to the root-covered plaza. I toss away the key. I head toward the concrete bench that encircles the tree. I walk among the penitents. It smells like fire and people. When I was the sacristan's assistant, I used to beg on God's behalf. Now, among these wretches, my new life begins: I beg for myself. Nobody denies me their blessing. Bells ring from other churches.

The Bengal Tiger

A WOMAN IS DANCING and a scream is heard. A woman is cleaning and a tiger appears. A woman is screaming because a tiger appears. A tiger is walking and a woman appears. A tiger eats up the woman that's dancing. A scream eats up the tiger that's cleaning. A dance screams up the woman that's tigering.

The husband gets home from work. The husband doesn't work. The husband goes to work because the tiger ate his wife. The husband flees his home, afraid of the tiger who ate his wife. The husband flees, afraid of the wife who ate the tiger. The husband flees, afraid of the police accusing him of being a tiger. (Switch to the past.)

The tiger was the woman's husband. The tiger was the husband's wife. It was a marriage of tiger and wife. Case in point: Tarzan and Cheeta (bestiality). The tiger and the woman—she was a dancer—used to work in a circus. That's where they met and that's where they fell in love. They were wed and they lived happily ever after. They were wed and they were slaves and ate graves. They were wed and they were blue and ate tulle. They were wed and they were atheists and ate yeast. They were wed and they did not eat. So, the starving tiger ate up the woman. The starving woman ate up the tiger husband. They weren't wed or together at all and they'd never even met. The tiger dreamed of the woman because he was hungry, and, in his dreams, he ate her up. The woman dreamed the husband was a tiger and the beast devoured her. The husband dreamed the woman was in love with a tiger, and, out of jealousy, he ate her up. (Switch to the present.)

The tiger looks at himself in a mirror and sees the man's reflection instead of his own. He eats him up. The woman looks at herself in a mirror but rather than her own reflection there's a hungry tiger staring at her. There is a moment of stillness, the tiger in the mirror blinks its calm feline eyes, and then it leaps out of the mirror with a ferocious roar and devours the woman. (Switch to the past.)

The tiger, the woman, and the husband were friends. They were living happily ever after and ate worms and plaster. The husband and the tiger were friends and they would eat women. The woman and the husband were friends and they would eat tigers. (Switch to the present.)

I'm the tiger who is thinking all this. The woman is Susana Chagal and the husband is Tiburcio Ginastera. I eat up Tiburcio (RIP), and kidnap Susana and bring her to Bengal. "Mr. and Mrs. Bengal Tiger invite you to a cocktail party to mourn among friends the life of Tiburcio Ginastera." (RSVP.)

I am Tiburcio who goes to Bengal to rescue his kidnapped wife from a dastardly tiger. I arrive in Bengal, capture the tiger, and bring him to the Buenos Aires circus, where I am the tamer and Susana the écuyère. We love each other and laugh at the poor tiger who is in love and encaged.

Sometimes, when I am feeling benevolent, I buy him a few pounds of horse meat. I do not hate the tiger: I understand him. Susana does not love him. Susana loves me.

The tiger is fed up with his relationship with the humans and he begins to hate Susana. A tiger claw to Susana's face! I poison the tiger (horse meat and cyanide). When Susana's in the operating room waiting for the plastic surgeon to operate on her mangled face she notices the doctor is a tiger. She screams. I enter the room. The first bars of the Fifth Symphony play: So, so, so, so, mi; fa, fa, fa, fa, re. Silence. We look at each other. The tiger doctor lunges at me and claws at my face. When I'm in the operating room I discover that Susana is the nurse and the doctor is Tiburcio Ginastera. I think of a tiger au gratin in a gray grotto and a grotesque and ungrateful groan takes the shape and sound of Susana's name. As in a dream, I realize that all of earth's surface is a mirror. Ergo, everything that happens happens simultaneously in reality and on another plane: the surface of the planet. The surface is the consciousness of the species. Actions are doubled. The surface is not a mirror. It's not the surface, it's the sky. The memory of the mirror. The mirror as memory. A tiger penetrates a mirror's abyss. The tiger's eyes are the mystery's mirrors. Susana looks at herself in a mirror and the mirror transforms her into a transparent being such that her reflection no longer appears. She evanesces before an evanescent mirror. The invisible woman. Invisible Susana. Invisible Tiburcio. Invisible me. The invisible tiger. "Tiger" and "Tiburcio" begin with "ti." "Sueño" and "Susana" start with "su." The only thing that exists in the world are the Bengal tiger's eyes. Reality is the image its eyes project. For an instant, when the tiger blinks, reality disappears.

I get rid of Tiburcio and the tiger. Heartbroken, my mind wanders. In this version, it's just Susana Chagal and I. Susana and I walk barefoot on a vast white beach, without speaking, without remembering, without thinking, without imagining, without anything but being, and the sea makes its global din and its water and its foam and its blows and its sounds vanish at our feet, and the night is bottomless, and the shellfish smell like a marine garden in the docile air, and the stars emit their cosmic hum, and Susana and I, unaware, are eternal in those instants having escaped from time forever. (Mankind will end up isolating instants just as they have isolated atoms. Instants will be bombarded with instantaneous reactors. And after they've been thoroughly studied, it shall be proven that instants are like small solar systems orbited by slow and infinitesimal satellites of eternity.)

Susana and I straddle a pair of equine instants and gallop along the beach because a tiger's devoured Tiburcio Ginastera and we must flee toward the happiness at the other end of infinity, where, unbeknownst to her and me, there awaits a beautiful and starving Bengal tiger, which, every time it blinks, extinguishes reality for an instant.

The Model

For "Mandrake and Lotus"

INTRODUCTION

The logic upon which our language is based forces us to accept a rather innocent order of causes and effects: the conventional before and after. So, as long as we use our current language, time will work in our stories like the waves of the sea beneath a child's drawing of a sailboat. But suddenly, what the child has drawn is the sea, and the ship serves only to prove it.

Perhaps this isn't a simple love story but rather a description of one of time's abominable jokes.

THE FACTS

My underwear was falling apart. This wasn't a recent discovery. At some point I had to start wearing swimming trunks, and eventually, I had to go commando. Although I've never been too convinced of underwear's indispensability, out of revolutionary laziness or conservative inertia, I decided I should buy some. Then again, I reasoned, the only thing that makes you question their usefulness is their absence.

A few months ago, I found myself with some money and nothing between my skin and my pants. I went into a store on Cabildo Street where they sold what I wanted most: underwear without elastic, made of striped and checkered fabric. Underwear, in short, that was nothing like the under-wear I've worn since I was a kid. This had two advantages: it concealed my inability to rebel, while also representing a kind of protest against my tendency to stall when it comes to fulfilling burdensome traditions.

The store was small and the salesmen were efficient, nu-merous, and homosexual. A parade of smiling young men were treating me like the guest of honor when I suddenly heard my name called—a bit blasphemously, I should say—by a surprised, almost joyful, feminine voice. As I told the salesmen to bag the underwear for me—two pairs with stripes and two with checkers—I turned around and found myself face-to-face with Etelvina. She is a tall, thin woman with sharp cheekbones, small teeth, long, coppery hair, a devious smile, and, to top it all off, a warm, thick voice.

I left with my purchase in one hand and the other on Etelvina's shoulder. I studied her profile but she looked straight ahead, never bestowing upon me the fullness of her smile. She was almost always smiling. She was wearing a horsehide coat, and I thought with bemused cynicism that surely the leather looked better on her than on the horse.

It was one of those bright winter mornings in Buenos Aires when the sun sparkles in the air and people's eyes and covers the sidewalks and the facades of the houses with a golden film of geometric patterns. (For me, the neighborhood of Belgrano, with its groves and granite streets, its shade and its silence, has always produced the same distrust as cemeteries. As a porteño, you're delighted that Belgrano exists, but to live in that neigh-borhood is to be permanently reminded of death; Belgrano is like Bécquer: romantic, morbid, and secretly corrosive.)

I suggested we go for coffee for one main reason: I wanted to see her face. She said no. We went to her house. Etelvina was very wealthy. She lived in one of those old mansions of indeterminate style that date back to the beginning of the century. The house was crowned with mansard windows, and though the foyer was perhaps a bit excessive, the splendid garden surrounding it was capable of remedying any architectural deficiency.

We drank Turkish coffee and, almost without either of us realizing it, began a ritual we'd follow every day: Etelvina left the room and returned in a completely different outfit. The first time she came back wearing purple pants and a silver blouse with long, wide sleeves. The combination of purple and silver reminded me of the ribbons on a funeral wreath. Crudely, I suggested she go dressed like that to a wake. From this absurd idea the game was born: she would change her clothes and I would come up with the ideal occasion for each outfit. Naturally, the idea evolved into increasingly subtle combinations.

Etelvina seemed to have an endless supply of coats, suits, dresses, furs, hats, shoes, and handbags. Every day we held a fashion show in which she was the only model and I was the only audience. My proposals were thoroughly analyzed, but if neither's points convinced the other, we'd get into heated arguments not devoid of passionate verbal violence.

I quickly became an expert in fashion and opined with sound reasoning. I don't know why we kept on playing. I've wondered if, at first, my secret and petty desire was not to exhaust her outfits and, one day, force her to confess that she had nothing left to wear.

Nevertheless, Etelvina's fantastic quantity of clothing led me to believe she must have a hidden workshop where hundreds of women, already half-blind, toiled sewing new garments so that we could continue our game. Sometimes I'd imagine a complicated system of elevators descending to underground passages whose walls were lined with miles of wardrobes filled with millions of garments. I even came to think that maybe I'd already been doomed to a circle of hell where I would pay for my wretchedness forever. I thought it might have something to do with the modesty of my underwear—the purchase of which had caused this condemnation—but I could never figure out the link between my reasonable garments and the lavish beauty of the silks, the furs, the organzas, the wools richly illuminated by subtle strands of silver, the most delicate tulles, the volatile gauzes embellished with perfect trim, the intricate embroideries. However, it didn't seem like hell because the incessant fashion show caused me displeasure, but rather because I glimpsed a hidden treachery in the unlimited versions of a single human being.

These feelings of doom arose while I waited for Etelvina to come back and enchant me with a new bathing suit, a new tailleur, or a new party dress. On the other hand, the joy I felt in her presence was also unlimited, which compensated for the interludes' dreary privations.

Etelvina was dazzlingly beautiful. Each fashion show—which usually lasted a couple of hours—was like touring a museum of marvelous paintings and miraculous sculptures. There was something so distant and magical in her sweetly smiling face that no one could ever tire of this game in which all possible forms of beauty were discovered but never repeated.

Over time I realized that, as a matter of fact, she wanted to give me her beauty in every imaginable circumstance and at every possible level. I remember Etelvina as if she were a village of women.

Our fashion shows were getting better and better. We created a spectacular Greta in *Ninotchka*, with a severe tailleur of tan tweed, and a tragic Michèle in *Port of Shadows*, with a black silk raincoat and a Cardin beret. Every bit as good was our version of Joan Fontaine in *The Constant Nymph*, where we made use of an almost adolescent outfit paired with a jabot blouse of very thin lace.

We perfected our performances with a mauve tulle deshabille that allowed us to create a very dignified Ophelia, transfigured by dementia, in the dim light of a Belgrano sunset that the trees perfumed with melancholy. Electra was the result of a great black velvet dress that Etelvina wore barefoot and mysteriously devoid of her delirious smile. I don't think there's ever been an actress capable of embodying Crommelynck's Carina with greater depth. For her, we created a four-piece outfit (two white pieces and two black) that, if worn in a room full of mirrors, would have given the impression of duplicating infinity.

Etelvina never looked at me as she modeled her outfits. Her eyes would get lost in a rapture that was more the result of surrender than concentration. My admiration was a waste of time because when I admired her, I could not love her. At times I wondered regretfully if a woman capable of combining all women could be the object of love, or if that itself was love's function: to sum up in one person all the creatures of the species. And so, amid the uneasiness that so much mystery caused me, I arrived at a form of self-dissolution in Etelvina that I'm not sure is what's conventionally called love, but which approached the limit of what I believe must be the experience of the absolute, or of mystical joy through ecstasy.

One afternoon our session ended somewhat dramatically. Etelvina became a character for whom—it was the only time this happened to me—I could not find a name or scene. My blood ran cold when I saw her appear in a white satin dress whose long tail followed her slow steps through the room like a trail of foam. A magnificent tiara gleamed on her high forehead and, in a hand covered by a very long glove, she carried a bouquet of white roses. As she passed, she stopped and looked at me with her deep and secret eyes. I think I saw her cry, but her smile moved me so much that I lowered my gaze. I didn't look up until I realized she was slowly walking away: down her back, her copper hair fell like a great tongue of fire.

I got up and left because I wanted to take the magic of those moments with me to savor in my most interior solitude.

The following afternoon I went back to Etelvina's house. I took a taxi and when I arrived at the front entrance, I was surprised to find that all the doors and windows were shuttered. It was as if a sudden rot had taken over the garden and the molding along the house's facade, which now seemed beset by rapid decay, and the lattices, which gave the impression of having been worn away by oxidation. In the marble staircase, in the rusty railings, everywhere, one could see the distressing presence of decline. That Bécquerian and sickly Belgrano I rejected had suddenly appeared in the house. It was strange, but I thought I might have refused to see things as they were for a long time, and that the splendor I had attributed to it up until that moment was related to Etelvina's health and beauty. I tried to keep seeing the house as I had always seen it: noble in its old age, carefully maintained, with its gates and shutters freshly painted, its gray but pristine and dignified moldings and balustrades, its burnished marbles and gleaming bronzes.

I rang the bell. A padlock secured a thick, rusty chain around the gate. I rang again, this time almost desperately. At last, an old woman came out. She was wrapped in a frayed and dun-colored flannel robe. Agitated, I asked her if Etelvina was home. I felt like the planet was spinning backwards or the air had been infused with shame. Everything was upside down.

"No!" shouted the old woman from the door. She ran across the withered garden to the gate. When she was in front of me, looking at me in horror, she shouted again, "Don't you know Etelvina died ten years ago! Why do you wish to disturb the dead?"

Only the velvety and radiant moss, which had grown over the patches of condensation, beautified the walls of the abandoned house. I realized that, horrified as I was, I could still remember a recent evening when Etelvina wore, behind the secret veil of her smile, a beautiful velvet cloak the color of moss and, underneath, a gauze dress with a deep neckline that revealed her firm and bountiful bosom.

I don't know if it was the mournful beauty of my voice, which promised no violence, or the burning pain in my gaze that persuaded the miserable old woman: a few minutes later I was crossing the marble path lined with dead bulbs and sparse brown grass. I explained that I'd been to the house before, that I loved Etelvina, that I wanted to see the room where in some still nameless way we'd loved each other at one moment in time: that it no longer mattered when Etelvina had died or when yesterday was. The old woman was wrapped in a magical form of absence: when she removed the chain, I smelled old age on her hands as I kissed them. I entered the house alone. The furniture was the same. Everything was covered with a thick layer of dust. The gilded harp was in the corner, its strings broken. I went to my usual chair. The furniture had developed a patina of resentful, creaking loneliness over the course of its prolonged disuse. I opened the squeaky lattices. I took a seat in my armchair, which smelled like a basement, a museum, a tomb, like death, and waited in vain for Etelvina. When I could see through my tears again, I noticed the floor (a parquet of rhombuses and dusty squares) was shining with the imprint of the trail Etelvina's white dress had left the previous afternoon. The bouquet of fresh roses was still on a side table, repeated in a foggy mirror.

The only thing I knew was that there, in that particular spot, I had loved her at one point in time. The only thing keeping me sane was the imprint of a white dress and a bouquet of roses that had begun to wilt.

I left at dusk. Time and death roamed the streets without cause or direction.

THE END

NOTE

I have only been truthful about one thing: Etelvina is dazzlingly beautiful. I met her a few years before our second encounter, which, in fact, did take place one morning while I was buying underwear on Cabildo Street. That same morning, we went to her apartment. Etelvina is poorer than a church mouse. Her meager wardrobe holds no more than a dozen garments of dubious taste. It's also true that we drank Turkish coffee. Afterwards we lay together brutally, as we would incessantly throughout our ferocious relationship.

After a few months of vulgar assiduity, of uninhibited afternoons and delirious nights, I was overcome by a painful weariness. A touch of horror and shame. Perhaps a hidden part of my being denounced myself as a traitor to the species. Anyone would feel that way if they voluntarily drowned themselves in the abjection of unbridled lust.

In addition to her frenzied lasciviousness, Etelvina lives in total chaos. She is disintegrating, soothing. Her limitless vanity and stupid pride became my allies. In her defects I found cause for my growing rejection. I realized they were the cracks through which I'd escape our sordid animality.

One afternoon she asked with her usual foolishness if I would ever write a story in which she was the protagonist. I think for the first time in my life I felt my blood boil from the fire of real anger. But then, suddenly, I saw a door open before my eyes: I told her categorically no, neither I nor anyone else could ever use a personality like hers to write anything. Certain her vanity would not take it, I gave false arguments based on alleged experiences.

Her eyes became loaded with different densities of hatred. This ended with curses, threats, insults, accusations, and all types of verbal torment. I left feeling liberated. I walked home with the joy, excitement, and sadness of someone who has tasted victory.

I packed a suitcase and that same night took the *Vapor de la Carrera* to Montevideo. I spent three weeks there working with Celas Ortiz on the staging of a young Mexican actor's latest play. I think I helped him solve a couple of problems. I went out with a girl who was doing the costumes and was on the verge of falling in love with her, but the memory of Etelvina haunted me in an ever more pressing way. I seemed to find her on every street corner: in cafés, on buses, in stores. In every woman, I found a gesture of hers, in every voice, an inflection that reminded me of her. In short: what always happens when someone is keeping their eye on an absence. I returned to Buenos Aires.

I led an almost calcified existence. I spent my days lying in bed. My loneliness was useless and heavy. Finally, I had to confess to myself that I couldn't live without Etelvina. I called her. She refused to speak with me. I called her again. The insults she hurled at me over the phone seemed to be the only ones left unsaid on the afternoon of our breakup.

Around that time, I received a letter from a poet who is active on the scene in Entre Ríos and who, for some inexplicable reason, holds me in high esteem. He announced that he was founding a literary magazine (surely in search of his own provincial prestige) and asked me if I'd do him the favor of submitting a piece for his publication. I asked him, in turn, to accept "Mandrake and Lotus," a story I told him I'd planned on writing for years, but that my meager economic means would undoubtedly postpone until after I was dead.

He ceremoniously and happily accepted my proposal without realizing the title was inspired by Mandrake and Lothar, two characters who have helped me ward off depression and sorrow ever since I was a little boy. (Wearing a cape, tails, and a top hat, Mandrake the Magician and his assistant Lothar (wearing shorts, a leopard skin shirt, and a fez) stroll along Fifth Avenue in New York City or the Via Veneto or traverse threatening African jungles or break into a meeting of the United Nations Security Council to disarm a demented evildoer and his band of international outlaws. And you end up thinking it's natural that clothing so absurd and out of season is as suitable for the jungle as it is for submarines.)

Once I'd pulled off my literary prank, I was sure I had everything I needed to get Etelvina back. I wrote the story "The Model" (modeling was Etelvina's failed vocation), and described our meeting just as it occurred. I named the character after her, of course, and I didn't forget the detail about the coffee. The oft-used theme of a woman who visits us from death seemed ideal. I presented my literary version of Etelvina, disguising each of our brutal unions with the metaphor of different outfits, as if each time we met she was magically the same and wonderfully different. In exchange for surrendering my cherished story, I demanded that my poet friend print it in his magazine's first issue. As soon as it was published, I sent Etelvina a copy along with a note. We started seeing each other again.

Now Etelvina and I are in an all-out battle. I think we're killing each other with sex, with our hatred disguised as love. We both know this ends with our death. I smell a whiff of gunpowder in her revolting mouth.

The CCC

THE DAY THE CCC on the corner of Neuquén and Donato Álvarez opened, my cousin (we call him Colorado because of his red hair) and I went into the café. I think we were their first customers. We chose the table on the right, in the chamfered corner. From there we could see the soft dip of Plaza Irlanda.

Colorado is rather quiet, whereas I tend to be long-winded. Since we were kids, we've shared the same room in what used to be my grandmother's house, and I remember my nightly ramblings being cut short by his sudden snoring. As I was saying, we walked into the CCC, and as soon as the only waiter appeared, we told him (I told him, to be precise) how nice the establishment looked. He replied dryly that it was the work of the architect Galíndez, and that all of the chain's locations were opening that same day.

We ordered coffee and dice. The morning was cool and the wan sunlight lit up even the corners of the café. Everything gleamed: the faucets, the chrome hangers, the pitchers, the glasses, the bottles, even the plastic-covered tabletops that cushioned the roll of the dice. Lots of chrome, lots of plastic, all as shiny as a new pin. So much so that it was almost uncomfortable.

Galíndez, somewhat perversely, had used the same blueprint for all the locations. As a result, identical CCCs were scattered across various parts of the city. Various but not different. The scattering was not done haphazardly. Each café was built in front of a plaza, and always kitty-corner to it. Thus, from the windows of any location (especially from those in the chamfered corners), the view was, with slight modifications, almost exactly the same.

You couldn't say our CCC had the charm of an old-timey café. A ventilation system prevented the smoke and the air from growing dense the way it used to. The waiter behaved more like a nurse than a servant. You'd order your coffee and make a comment about yesterday or tomorrow's match, and you'd get a look instead of an answer (Colorado described this look as "professional," although neither of us ever considered the corresponding profession). And yet, this look of the waiter's, even though it didn't answer, was enough to satisfy. In other words, just saying nothing would have been rude, but saying nothing and giving you that look was a way, albeit vague, of answering.

As always, Colo and I played generalas[1] for a couple of hours. We played for cups of coffee. It's just another way to pass the time, especially now that we're retired: we'd whistle, play (almost silently), drink a few coffees, and look at the plaza. It was all very peaceful because in the morning nobody else went to the CCC. Apparently, in the afternoon, teenagers from the trade school on Gaona Street filled up the place. But we always got there around ten and left by twelve, twelve fifteen.

---

1. Dice game similar to Yahtzee

About twenty days ago, on a Tuesday, when we were returning home for lunch, Colorado opened his mouth. This was unusual. "What do you think about going to a different CCC one of these days?" he asked. Colo may be quiet but every time he speaks, he has his reasons. I was almost mortified because the idea hadn't occurred to me. I objected: "Why would we if ours is six blocks away?"

"I don't know," my cousin replied. I kept quiet. We got home and ate lunch. I'm not exaggerating when I say both my sister and Colorado's sister are the best cooks in Buenos Aires. Everything they make is simple, nothing fancy, but their ravioli is ravioli and their matambre is matambre. We ate and went to lie down for a while. We both read the newspaper; I read *La Nación* and my cousin reads *Clarín*. As I mentioned before, we've always shared the same room. I still comment on what I'm reading (like I did when we were kids), but he never answers me. Suddenly I hear him snoring and I realize it's better to turn over and go to sleep.

His idea had mattered to me more than I thought. As soon as I woke up, I had the suspicion, but not the certainty, of having dreamed about the CCCs. What I am sure of is this: something the waiter said on opening day returned to my mind. I'd never thought about the comment nor was I even aware of having registered it. It was his "warning" (and I wasn't even sure what compelled me to call it a "warning") that all the locations were identical and had opened the same day. I mentioned it to Colo and he corroborated my observation. But he couldn't explain why he remembered the comment as having been made in a subtly threatening way, either. In any case, we both seem to have retained it as a veiled threat even though when the waiter made it, there didn't seem to be anything aggressive in his tone.

The next morning, we left the house at the same time we did every day, around half past nine. When we reached the corner of Biedma and Neuquén, my cousin made one last attempt.

"So, you're not coming?"

"No. I'm going to our café," I told him curtly, as if my choosing independence made me bigger.

"OK," replied Colo with his permanent air of indifference and resignation.

I watched him get on a bus and I continued on my way. I sat down at our usual table and—I have to admit—I couldn't help but feel offended. Suddenly I was in a very bad mood. I feel this way whenever Colo acts unilaterally. I feel betrayed by him. I'm a creature of habit, whereas he can easily change his routines as if they were nothing. This is what I was thinking about when Colorado appeared. He burst in like a hurricane. His face was transformed and I saw terror in his eyes.

"What are you doing here?" he asked me under his breath in exasperated disbelief.

"What are *you* doing here?" I countered, surprised.

"Didn't you tell me you didn't want to go to another CCC?"

"Don't play dumb," I replied, irritated.

Colo remained poker-faced, but when the waiter approached our table, he seemed like he was about to faint.

"Do you feel sick?" I asked, genuinely concerned.

"No," he answered. "I'm fine, I'm fine."

Colo ordered coffee but didn't want to play. It was half past eleven and I suggested we go back home. We left. I walked out first. I waited for a moment on the sidewalk, but Colo, who had been right behind me, suddenly disappeared. I went back inside, or rather, I poked my head in and looked around the café. Colo wasn't there. "He left," said the waiter. I decided my cousin was going nuts and walked home by myself. My sister and my cousin (Colo's sister) were surprised to see me come back alone. I didn't say a word and went into the bedroom. Half an hour later my cousin arrived.

"Where'd you go?" he asked me, half whispering, half shouting.

"The same place as you!" I answered angrily.

"Let's eat," said Colo. It was almost an order. "Afterward I need to think about something." Then he added, "You went to the CCC on Neuquén, didn't you?"

"Of course," I said, alarmed. I was beginning to suspect that something was really off. "Weren't we together? What I don't understand is where you went when we left."

"OK," said Colo with his eyes closed. "I'd better skip lunch. Now let me think. We'll talk later."

The women and I ate lunch. When the four of us aren't together everything goes upside down. It must be from habit and because we're starting to get old. The thing is, I could hardly take a bite even though Wednesdays are lentils with red chorizo. And the way they make it at home, it's my favorite food in the world.

I went back to the bedroom and found Colo sitting on the edge of his bed.

"Come in here," he said. "I've already figured everything out. Tomorrow you can see for yourself. We're in a trap."

"You're sort of going nuts, aren't you," I said.

"Listen to me," he said, and he explained to me what happened.

Colo got on the bus at Neuquén and Biedma, where we parted. He went straight to the CCC in Plaza Lezica. When he arrived, he was surprised to see me. He went in and we had a conversation that he repeated to me verbatim. It was the same one I'd had with him when I saw him walk into our usual CCC on Donato Álvarez and Neuquén. When Colo saw the same waiter approaching, he turned pale because his theory fell to pieces. He thought I'd been playing a joke on him by pretending not to know that I'd also gone to Lezica. When we ("the other you and the real me") left the CCC in Lezica, my cousin said I seemed to disappear. The opposite of what had happened to me.

Colo came to the following conclusion: every day, in every CCC, he and I were being replicated simultaneously. Tomorrow I could see for myself. He would sit at our usual table at our usual CCC. I would take a cab and go to whichever location I felt like without telling my cousin. I could get out, or I could stay in the cab and go to another location. In every single one of them, I would see Colo sitting at the same corner table. I could go in and talk to a fake Colo. The real Colo would then repeat the exact same words to me when I arrived at our CCC.

And so it was. The test was performed. It came out just like Colo said it would. We were filled with dread. I was horrified by the idea that every time I had a cup of coffee there were several Rolandos (my name is Rolando) raising their hands simultaneously. It made me sort of nauseous to think that every time I had a full house of aces and fours there

were a bunch of Rolandos—as many as the CCC has locations—having my exact same experience. I felt like throwing
up but I contained myself. Every day, when we went into
the café on Donato Álvarez and Neuquén, a bunch of other
Colorados and Rolandos walked into the rest of the CCCs.

The idea that we were no longer unique provoked an intolerable fear. The multiplicity, however, occurred exclusively
inside the CCCs. We came to the following conclusions: 1)
Our presence in one of the locations caused the simultaneous
replication in all the others. 2) If we killed off one of the replicas it would cause the death of all of them. 3) We wouldn't
be able to kill them "from the outside" because if we didn't
go to our café, we wouldn't be in any of them. 4) If Colorado
shot the Rolando in Lezica or Belgrano, he would kill all the
Rolandos, but I would die too, even if I was in "our" CCC.
5) The only way to guarantee that we'd destroyed them all
was for Colo and me to commit suicide in the CCC at Donato Álvarez and Neuquén, therefore causing the simultaneous
suicides of all our replicas. (We didn't care for this option.)

Finally we found another way out. I don't know if I
already mentioned that my cousin is retired from the state
arms manufacturer Fabricaciones Militares, where he was
Deputy Chief of the materials warehouse, and that until last
year I worked in the famous Escasany jewelry store. This
information would explain where we got the explosives and
who made the bomb.

Yesterday we planted it. We played generalas like we do
every day. At ten past twelve, we left. We sat on a bench in
the plaza and at twelve thirty we watched the CCC on Neuquén and Donato Álvarez turn to rubble.

In the sixth edition of *La Razón*—which we never bought, except for yesterday—the news came out: all of the CCC's locations had been destroyed simultaneously. The newspaper said that "mere criminal hands" could not have carried it out and that it was undoubtedly the work of an extremist organization familiar with "the most advanced commando-style techniques." The newspaper added that "it was no accident" that the arrival of a well-known American industrialist—the famous chain's majority owner—happened to coincide with the terrorist act. We chose yesterday to plant the bomb; maybe Colorado was too exact in his choice—I'd even say hellbent—but I swear that I, at least I, did not have the slightest suspicion of that gentleman's arrival.

The Singer

FEARLESSLY MEMORY VENTURES to places that matter not because they're from the past but because they're hidden now and no one would voluntarily draw back those tulle curtains full of sleeping vermin were it not out of innocence or love because it's the only way to go down the paths of mystery one afternoon it was pretty cold and getting late my uncle luciano came in and announced what we at home already knew the singer had died he said two words his name and the verb luciano was thin and dramatic it was definitely dark by the time he got there from the radio we already knew he'd died but it took luciano's voice for us to feel our devastation it's always someone else who helps you see the scope of your pain solitude is clumsy i was too young to understand that you take the most recent death and add the anguish you feel from all the deaths that have preceded it and death had already visited me before so i added the singer's death i think we all did the same thing we combined the deaths and placed them on the singer at home a guilt that wasn't mine used to float around the house the adults felt guilty about everyone who'd died and also because the singer had died in a faraway country possibly forgotten possibly disputed by luciano himself not to mention everyone else at home possibly everyone on our block in our neighborhood in the city doubted the singer died in the fire we did not even get his body back in death he was turned to ashes and returned to the city which only now realized it adored and worshipped him and was even grateful to him what do i know because singing is serious business and it sort of made us real if you want to know the truth when the singer died in my house all i saw was shame no one dared admit that perhaps they felt a sort of love for the singer although anyone could have said that without being untruthful and it was the way he spoke and not so much what he said his tone his accent became how we saw and loved our fellow man the singer was now a presence simply because he'd died and would be so forever with that brusque and assured quality that death has in its foreverness and since we can no longer see those who ride that trackless train between the stars and who knows maybe they're below and not above as everyone says thinking about aboves and belows it has nothing to do with places but with the fact that they are gone forever and one either puts up with not knowing or joins whatever group they can out of loneliness what's certain is the singer was dead for the city and me forever or rather for never because for singers above means going around and around and around and around again being given voice by the country men women and even children who will grow up so that his voice if it isn't in vain not everyone believed it some of us thought he'd survived and was still alive in spain almost thirty years later a spaniard pretended to be him but it was just some crazy bum the singer died that winter day and everything changed when the singer died the country changed and we began to seek him in our memory and give him life because there had to be a reason he was dead forever after him all the singers began to die just like him because he'd come up with the song by that i mean how

singers live and die the caricature puts the symbol at risk the
same way the leader is always disfigured by foppish imitations
just like during carnival a mishmash of admiration and helpless-
ness and at the end of the day even though everything is human
not everything is admirable at my house that night it was like we
were in silent mourning and it was all whispers i don't remember if it was that same day or the one after or the next our grief
lasted a long time we listened to abel fleury on the radio playing
the song cien guitarras at luna park in memory of the singer
as if the singer wasn't already pure memory what i mean is his
death brushed my home like the wing of a great bird dropping
a little bit of ash with every wingbeat but it swept through the
house and my house was everyone's house and listen these are
not empty words for good reason it was buenosaires everything
that happened happened there even the fig tree and the jasmines
the police and so many things that transcend mere telling from
that day on we heard him sing on the radio every morning and
every night and there was no use i was sure he was singing from
the grave and from then on death was mixed with life and my
goodness how blind we were at least the radio was there to wash
away the guilt at least the fig tree in the yard still bore figs and i
began combing my hair with tragacanth i think so i could look
like everyone else who also wanted to look like the singer como
cualquier cacatúa² i wore a blue tie with white stripes like the
ones he used to wear and when we went to the cinema and saw

2. Literally, "like any cockatoo." In Lunfardo, a cacatúa is someone insignificant
or mediocre. Bonomini is almost certainly referencing the tango "Corrientes y
Esmeralda" by Celedonio Flores, which has the line "en tu esquina rea cualquier
cacatúa sueña con la pinta de Carlos Gardel" ("on the corner of skid row where all
the nobodies dream of having Carlos Gardel's looks").

him moving and talking and above all singing we believed he was still alive and that everything had been a dream and one day he'd return to tell us about the hospital where he'd stayed where they'd healed his burns and fortunately his face was untouched by flames to be honest i think we were never the same after the day the singer died every morning on the radio we'd hear his voice fill the courtyard and climb the branches of the fig tree and every night his voice mixed with my own and everyone else's who heard him sing because his singing changed us for the better and changed death itself and kept on changing us it happened in july i will never forget i was playing hopscotch under the fig tree in the courtyard at my grandmother's house i think it was cold and i was wearing a wool jacket the color of tea with milk when luciano arrived and announced his death nobody was surprised but we all realized this death was more painful and permanent than we had previously thought let's be honest the person who delivers the news does so with a certain pride as if they were responsible for having invented it luciano felt the death he announced belonged to him i'm sure he walked quickly beneath the plátano trees rehearsing the tone he would ultimately be unable to recreate because he was undone by what had happened and because sometimes words climb into our voices so that what matters is not the words themselves but the voice that utters them to embody desperation or joy or secret confession silence or scream the radio said it all someone else didn't need to tell us directly for it to be true it took luciano's voice for the singer to really truly forever die it was in july and i was playing outside when i heard him sing mibuenosairesquerido everyone started to think the city was querido that's how it happened that's how the singer died once and for all

Theories

MY COUSIN'S RIGHT WHEN she says I'm full of theories. I always tell her whichever one I've just come up with. I don't know if it depends on her mood or the theories themselves, but sometimes she listens in silence, her brow furrowed, her eyes like an uninterested cat's as she makes little drawings with her pencil, and other times she dies laughing.

When my theories don't interest her much, she says, "You'd better see a doctor because I think you're going nuts."

I couldn't give two hoots (as my grandfather says) or a fig (as my Aunt Celina says). Some theories I can't tell her. They're very complex and it's as though they were woven with black thread in the dead of night. What is there to say when you have a theory like that?

So I say, "Jacinta, I have one but I can't tell you it."

Without looking up from her notebook, she asks, "Why not?"

"Because it's woven with black thread."

"Great," she snaps. "Are you going to let me study or not?"

I shut up. Then, all of a sudden, I think about the theory and can't stop laughing. Jacinta looks up at me and she laughs, too.

"You're so crazy!" she says.

She pretends not to care. Since she's two years older than me, she tries to act like an adult and pretend my theories don't matter to her. But they do matter to her. For example, when I told her the one about the fig tree, she kept quiet, as usual, and then went back to reading her book. A little while later, though, after we'd finished our homework, she went out to the backyard and started looking at the fig tree. She stretched out on one of the wooden folding chairs and just stared at it without saying a word. When I told her my theory about the word "temptation" (which was the same as my theory about the patch of dirt around the vine), I found her the next day—I remember it was a Sunday—kneeling by the vine, looking at it, and sniffing around like a puppy. She was checking to see if what I'd said was true: that the patch of dirt concealed a well. And so on and so forth. When I told her my theory about crazy people having their craziness stuck in their hair, she started brushing her hair twenty times a day. When I told her the one about cats being able to see colors, she'd change her blouse every twenty minutes and sit in front of Celina's cat.

On winter afternoons, the smell of pencil sticks to my hands and face. From this a theory could arise, but faced with the temptation I usually try to fight it because otherwise everything would become a theory. The smell of graphite, however, strikes me as important, and could lead to a good one. I know from experience that, in these cases, all you have to do is wait. Suddenly and inevitably, the theory will just appear.

And although it's extremely difficult for me, I try not to think about the theories, which is like having theories about theories. Once, for example, I came up with the idea of giving each theory a color. Another time, I thought of classifying them into groups: air, fire, water, and earth. Naturally, I was too lazy to go through with it. It'd be like drawing a map of a nonexistent country, with names for its rivers and mountains and cities. You can come up with a million ways to make a theory seem more convincing, but there's not much fun in it. It's impossible to invent something infinite.

One night, while I was lying in bed before falling asleep, I started listing all the theories. But when I was sure I'd thought of them all, I'd remember another. I eventually fell asleep thinking of the one about the melon seeds, which is one of the most entertaining. It's impossible to make a complete list of all the theories because you just end up laughing your head off. Every time I try to remember them all, I end up having to stuff my mouth with my sheets so I don't wake Jacinta, who sleeps in the bed next to mine. Sometimes, I try to list the names of the theories without thinking too much about them, but that is also impossible. For example: the one about the seeds, the one about hair, the one about crazy women and their hats, the one about gas pumps, the one about insects, the one about the fig tree, the one about the word "temptation," the one about bleach, the one about watching someone sleep, the one about glass when it's cold, the one about cats, the one about the mask (which Jacinta ended up smashing and flushing down the toilet), the one about rain on a tin roof, the one about birds that fall belly-up when they die, the one about drops of water that look like mirrors. The whole thing gets so complicated that you decide to either fall asleep or invent a new one before you can remember them all.

Today, after lunch, we were doing our homework. I began to contemplate the birds on the curtains. It seemed like at any moment they would fly off their embroidered branches. I was certain that if I kept on thinking about them, I would end up putting together a new theory. Suddenly, I couldn't not tell Jacinta about the one I came up with last night, even though I knew perfectly well that if I somehow managed to explain it to her, I'd undoubtably be exposed.

"I have a theory," I told her, unable to stop myself.

"A new one?" she asked, not looking up and starting to draw little pictures with her pencil.

"Yes, but it's almost like it's made of thread."

"So, you're not going to tell me it."

"I don't think so."

"It's probably really stupid."

"Well, I guess I'll shut up then."

"No. Tell me," she said, unable to hide her curiosity.

"Here it is: when you're dreaming, the room you're dreaming in turns into the place you're dreaming about."

"OK."

"And everything you dream about happens in that room. If you dream about a horse, there's a horse in the room. If you dream about a mountain full of dogs, there's mountain and it's full of dogs."

"OK."

"But when you open your eyes, everything disappears because dreams are like theories made of thread."

"OK."

"But what happens," I asked with disgust, "when two people sleep in the same room and dream at the same time?"

"What happens?" asked Jacinta, lifting her head and staring at me.

"What happens is you get into each other's dreams. And seeing as I think my theories are dreams I've had then suddenly remembered, it now occurs to me that maybe my theories are actually yours. Get it?"

"Yes," Jacinta replied. She went pale but kept drawing in her notebook as if I hadn't found her out.

The only thing that makes me horribly sick is the thought that maybe everything, absolutely everything, is nothing more than one of Jacinta's theories.

The Report

This junta has just assumed power without spilling a single drop of blood, thanks to the professionalism of my comrades in arms, who, in supporting me, have demonstrated a true spirit of sacrifice, faith in the Revolution, and love for the Fatherland.

This, Officers, was no improvised Revolution. The men with whom I will share the responsibilities of governing were, like me, imprisoned for five years by arbitrary mandate of the overthrown tyrant. In those five years of meditation and introspection, the philosophy behind our movement was conceived, and if I may speak personally, I was finally able to give shape to an intuition that's haunted me ever since I was a little boy.

After my personal awakening, I confronted the indoctrination phase. Faith instilled me with the capacity to persuade, and through patient teaching I was able to convert my comrades in arms and misfortune into true apostles of the doctrine. Like any universal upheaval, this doctrine has been revealed by supernatural powers to which this junta humbly submits, and so completely, may I add, that we will not hesitate to destroy any and all potential enemies using all of the equipment, techniques, and weapons at the Institution's disposal.

The purpose of this meeting is to inform the senior chiefs and officers about the basics of our philosophy. As you will soon see, our movement is not merely national, but universal.

I want to clarify, however, that this philosophy will obscure and hide and deny itself to the mind of anyone who tries to elucidate it using traditional logic for the simple reason that they are using an inadequate resource.

In logistics, we learn to use resources in a way that maximizes their operational efficiency and functionality. If we think using old techniques, we will only arrive at old ideas. To grasp our philosophy, we will need to resort to new ways of thinking. I am well aware that, from a semantic point of view, this report contains an essential contradiction. However, for didactic and practical reasons, in this first gathering, I have decided to use ordinary means (in this case ordinary language) to announce the new scope of our governmental theory.

This is just the beginning of the indoctrination that you, gentlemen, need in order to support us in the revolutionary work. Starting today, we will meet for two hours every morning at 7:30 a.m. until the officer corps is well acquainted with our theory. Unexcused absences will be considered treason against the Fatherland.

Here, in broad strokes, is the theory of the Revolution:

I have come to the conclusion that time is in reverse. From this it follows that God is the consequence of reality. In other words, that which will happen has, step by step, been creating what is and what was. What I mean is, six comes before five. This is not, gentlemen, a reversal of fatalism. Strictly speaking, what I am telling you now is not a theory but a testimony.

Let's face it, History is prediction and clairvoyance is History. Heroism is nothing more than a certain type of act that crystallizes without knowing its necessity, its likelihood, its consequences. Every action comes before the dilemma that resulted in choice. The firing squad precedes the betrayal.

The universe began with the Apocalypse and shall end with Genesis. A man shall kill his brother. His parents shall disobey. The mother shall become the man's rib. Innocent and left alone in Paradise, the man shall turn to dust. Then darkness shall come and God shall live in the Glory man hath created for Him.

Human senses function like mirrors, hence our error in the way we judge time. A man in front of a mirror is an inverted man: the left is to the right and the right is to the left. If a man walks toward a mirror, it will depict the trajectory from its depths to the walker. Thus, the senses. Thus, the traditional version of things. One of man's most profound dramas is that he can never see himself. I am not speaking in metaphors when I say that man is tragically fallen inside the mirror. His anguished inability to see himself forces him to trust in precisely that which will inexorably betray him. But I, gentlemen, am not anti-mirror. I am not anti-mirror because thanks to its coherent version, its repeated claim, its consistent language, the mirror reveals our truth to us. Strictly speaking, we have no right to call something traitorous if all it's ever done is lie. In fact, I propose we make the mirror our species' flag, because in it we have found the key to our destiny.

Revolutionary truth forces us to use a new form of logic. In a way, I have tried to state this fact before. Once the indoctrination period is over, the use of decadent Aristotelian logic will be considered treason to the Fatherland. Today's socioeconomic systems, both those of free enterprise and those of nationalization, adhere to precepts based in decadent logic. The Revolution, as you will see in report number twenty-nine next Sunday, February 2, utilizes other elements. The dramatic rise of identity, for example, which has caused so much damage especially in the world of finance, will be supplanted by the rise of infuturation, which the Minister of Revolutionary Logic will soon discuss. Who can think today that *a* is equal to *a*? Who can defend the clumsy idea that the first *a* in "Ana" is equal to the second *a* in "Ana"? And what of "banana," where each *a* assumes such a wildly different function? Each revolutionary *a* will rise to its appropriate height according to the activity that each *a* is assigned for the greatness of the cause. The hour of the Republic has arrived. The Revolution will create poets, philosophers, and painters so that they in turn can sow a new nation from the seeds of these Glad Tidings. This will come to pass when artists look to the future to write their songs; to the future and to the past, but to the real future and the real past, not the current past and current future!

I, a mere soldier tasked with governing the destinies of the people and the race, salute the free creators of the new Fatherland and the new confraternity of nations inspired by the revelation made to me: time is in reverse.

Gentlemen, beware: the aberration at the heart of the most patiently constructed and syntactically perfect sentences is masked by the fraudulent veracity of the current logic. Seemingly innocent, some rogue from the opposition will declare: "Time moves forward," and it will all seem seductively true, strictly systematic, and coherently expository. But that is treason! Plain and simple, time is in reverse.

This is how things must be in accordance with the new logic that reproduces the truth: time is in reverse, and whoever denies it: may God and the Fatherland have mercy on their souls!

Having already assumed power, which gives me the soothing feeling of its limits, I only wish to persuade. Power opens two paths: imposition or persuasion. That's why I insist the officer class allow itself to be persuaded. I have no other mission. This is my destiny, and one I assume with self-sacrificing faith in the Supreme Truth. We will get there by any means necessary.

Once the indoctrination stage and the revolutionary trainings are complete, we will have to make the sacrifice of temporarily walking away from our specific posts. Everyone, according to their capacity, will occupy a position in the administration of the State. What is the main objective of the second revolutionary stage? To create a great Ecumenical Council in which men of science, philosophers, artists, and mathematicians from all over the world will participate. A Great Permanent Assembly of the world's dignitaries, destined to put into practice the consequences of our discovery.

We have an enormous task ahead of us. Our eminent lawmakers will be tasked with rewriting the legislation. Mathematics, once adjusted to this new and ultimately truthful way of living, will lead us to surprising miracles.

Philologists will need to provide us with a modern language. Perhaps when we travel, we will call "arrivals" "departures," and "departures" "arrivals." Perhaps the year will begin in December and end in January. A great collective task of sensory rearrangement will accompany the Government and the Assembly.

Let's say it once and for all: in the future, mankind was immersed in the most endearing error a present mind can c onceive. The past awaits us with open arms: toward it, we throw ourselves with our hearts full of faith in God, the source of all reason and justice. The path of the people is a backward path that goes forward, in a time that comes from the future and will end in the past, because the time of our countrymen more than path is time, and more than time is path.

And before we intone our sacred Hymn, I invite you to pledge allegiance to the struggle for Revolution, which will lead us to the great destiny we are called to fulfill in concert with all the other nations of the Globe.

The Last One

"They camp at the foot of the embankments and then it can be seen that they carry in their bags leftovers from home: kitchen utensils, blankets to sleep on, plates to eat off. They sleep together like animals because the night is too powerful for the soul and the grief; but the next morning they leave quietly, one by one. It is as if God is lacking in their person."

—Ezequiel Martínez Estrada, translated by Alain Swietlicki

IT WAS ABOUT SEVEN O'CLOCK. From atop the embankment, the man with the blond beard looked up at the red sun on the horizon, and the sun crept into his beard like a vibrant varnish that made his face sparkle. He turned his back to the sunset and descended the green slope.

"Evening," he said.

"Evening," replied the man with the gray beard.

Their conversation finished, they went their separate ways. Their bags marked the spot where they would meet back up again. They returned with their hands full of twigs, branches, and straw and lit the fire.

The man with the gray beard took out a bottle of water and a little kettle. The other had crackers, maté, yerba, and a bombilla.[3] The man with the gray beard took a while to remove something else from his bag. It wasn't that he hesitated; he couldn't seem to find it. At last, while the blond was filling the kettle with water from the bottle, the old man pulled out a packet with a greasy wrapper. When he'd removed the

---

3 Maté is a traditional South American herbal drink, typically prepared by pouring hot water over dried yerba maté leaves in a calabash gourd (also called a maté) and consumed with a metal straw (bombilla).

paper, he revealed its contents and looked at his companion with defiant, laughing eyes.

"Salami," said the blond, who was much younger. His smooth, inexpressive voice was meant to signify his familiarity with the contents, so theatrically displayed, of the old man's package. "If you want," he offered.

"Uh-huh," replied the man with the blond beard, and he placed the kettle on the fire.

From his bag, the young man exhumed an olive-green military blanket hardened with stains and softened from use. He spread it out in his arms to examine it and laid it on the ground next to him. Then he threw his hat on top of it, revealing his bicolored forehead. The mark left by the sweatband drew a horizon over his eyes: above it, up to his hairline, his skin was thin, white, and smooth; below it, his skin was hard, reddish, porous, punished by sun and air. He leaned back against the foot of the slope while he waited for the water to heat. He closed his eyes and took a deep breath, his face toward the sky.

The old man continued rummaging through his bag.

The pampa closed in on these two men who had never met before and had hardly exchanged a word because almost everything was understood. The sunset was all theirs. Before their eyes, the horizon began to blur into an impenetrable mass of shadows. The smell of the earth at night was already creeping through the air, but they knew they would forget it the moment the sky revealed its stars. They drank maté. The young man was in charge of brewing it. From time to time, they added a splash of cold water to the kettle and twigs to the fire. The old man with the gray beard took a knife from his belt and split the salami in two. He skewered one half on the tip of his knife and offered it to the young man with the blond beard.

They ate the hardened meat and threw the greasy wrapper into the fire. For an instant, quick, high flames engulfed the kettle.

"Did you stop by Nájera's bar?" asked the old man with measured indifference.

"Yes."

That was all the old man wanted to know. A deep sigh of relief made his eyelids slowly close. Nájera's bar was to the south. The young man, then, had not walked along the train tracks, as he had, but had come cross-country. He couldn't have seen anything.

The old man also took off his hat. The little flames of the fire made lights and shadows dance across the wrinkles of his face.

"Well . . ." said the young man, insinuating a goodnight.

"What, you're going to sleep?" asked the old man anxiously. The young man lifted his head with a quick movement and looked at him sternly, with astonishment, as if the old man had said something insolent. The young man's swift, withering look struck the old man's face like a whip. Not even the night's shadows softened the fury in the young man's eyes. It had been many years since anyone had caused him offense by taking an interest in him. He laid his head back on the ground and pulled the military blanket around his torso as if his legs didn't belong to him. The old man registered the look, felt the snap, but did not flinch. He brewed the maté now, and for himself alone. After drinking three or four, and knowing that the man with the blond beard was not yet asleep, he offered him one.

"You don't want the last one?" he asked. His tone evinced his desire for reconciliation and excluded neither humor nor humility.

"Well, no," replied the young man, without departing entirely from his reverie.

You could hear and feel the pampa's invisible little animals. Insects and rodents traced swift and futile lines in the air and the earth. All toward the void. Toward nowhere. Vanishing. To feel alive.

The young man's reply was sweet. The old man forgot the sternness of his gaze and dared to continue.

"Did you hear anything at Nájera's place?"

"They want to put up a fence around a pasture in La Estefanía."

"Will there be work enough for two?"

"Enough for four."

"Is that so?" said the old man.

La Estefanía was about thirteen miles away. Just past the village.

"Bah!" exclaimed the old man after thinking for a few moments.

"What?" said the young man.

"Nothing, my friend, it's just that at any moment they could also find you dead on the side of the tracks."

"You as in me?"

"It's a figure of speech."

The young man raised his eyebrows without opening his eyes, like someone concentrating to recover a distant memory or perceive a very subtle scent. He thought about the old man's words, but since he couldn't get a grip on them, he explained, not without a certain harshness:

"Listen, sir: if you don't mind, I'd like to get some sleep."

"Go to sleep, go to sleep," replied the old man, and he began to empty the maté of its damp and saturated yerba.

Darkness fell upon the young man's eyelids.

The old man leaned against the slope, rested his head in his open hand, and stared in rapture at the young man's serene face, barely illuminated by the embers.

The old man's eyes: everything else was night. All was blind pampa, because the stars were so high that they appeared alien.

A few hours passed. The young man slept face up, hugging himself. The old man didn't sleep. He kept the fire alive so as not to be all alone. He didn't think. Behind the gray hairs of his mustache and beard there wandered a faint smile, especially when he added twigs to the fire. At about half past three he adjusted his hat, took off his rope-soled shoes, and shook them to remove any pebbles that might have slipped in. Then he put them back on and set off carrying his bag. He left his kettle next to the maté and the bombilla. Before climbing the embankment, he took one last look at the young man.

As soon as he'd reached the train tracks, he headed toward the village, toward La Estefanía.

"He won't wake up until the five o'clock train goes by," said the old man to himself, and he laughed mischievously.

The night was now drawn in a glittering pattern of four straight lines: the stars burnished the railroad tracks that split the pampa's circular immensity into two lonely halves.

It had been a long time since the old man had felt so happy. He'd probably kept the fire alive so his happiness wouldn't be diluted in the vastness of the night. "Let's see," he said to himself, "What did I do tonight? What did I do? Very simple. I took care of the blond guy." A childish laugh shook him. "I took care of the poor guy, and on top of that I left him the kettle, which was almost new." He laughed again with innocent glee.

The old man knew that, as the night progressed, he would lose that happiness, and he began to slow his gait to put off its disappearance. "It was good not to sleep a wink and take care of him, the poor thing," he said to himself. Full of joy, he hauled his bag and his old age, new almost to the experience of happiness. The gravel he walked on had been invaded and taken up by weeds. The night was cool. The train advanced in the distance like a rising star on the horizon. With his bag on the ground, he waited for the monster to whoosh past him. He watched it go by and continued his solitary march. After a while, the night dissolved into a gray half light and the stars began to fade in the sky. The smile on his face dissolved as well. The day and his memory cleared up at the same pace. As if until that moment the pampa and his ability to remember had been cloaked in the same shadows. What he remembered dawned over the plains of his memory, not to warm them and vivify his heart, but rather to freeze his burdened existence. Dawn lit the planetary wrinkles that traveled his face.

The previous afternoon he had been walking the same direction. He could only see the slope of the south-facing embankment. As usual, he was walking at the edge of his thoughts when he saw a man lying face down at the foot of the slope. He realized the man wasn't sleeping by how still he was. The old man descended with quick, short steps.

It was around four in the afternoon and the sun was still beating down. Birds had been circling the area for a little while now. Just to complete a sort of ritual, he lifted the man's head by his hair. The head was docile and gave way as if the force he'd used had been excessive, like when you lift an empty glass that you think is full. The dead man's dry eyes were two opaque pebbles. In his right hand, he held the knife he had used to viciously slit his own throat.

"He'll be eaten by birds," he thought. "I have to bury him." But then he hesitated. "What if they see me? The best thing to do is leave. But what if they find him? They'll blame me. I'd better go to Nájera's bar and tell them. They won't believe me! What if I start to bury him and someone shows up? And even if I don't bury him or say anything, when they find him, they'll find out who's been around, and they'll end up accusing me because they'll suspect me for not having reported it." He felt like he'd fallen into a trap. Despite being in the middle of the pampa, he had the bitter certainty that a cage was closing in on him. He unbuttoned the collar of his shirt. "Maybe I'd better go into town and call the police." But he corrected himself immediately. "Never! Nothing could be worse. Who's going to believe I didn't kill him? They'll say I did it to steal something from his bag, or over a fight." He sat down beside the dead man. He had met him two nights before. He was quiet and generous. He had slept like this, as he did presently, face down. They spent the night together, and at one point the dead man uttered some incomprehensible words: "One day they could also find you dead on the side of the tracks." The old man didn't understand and thought he was talking in his sleep or out of exhaustion.

"They won't believe me. Nobody will believe me. If someone comes along when I'm burying him, it'll be even worse. Someone can always appear at any moment in the desert. People sprout from the earth like unexpected trees, like unforeseen and pastless animals. All of a sudden there's someone next to you, or behind you. You look around and there's nobody there. The horizon is empty, but as if by miracle, a witness emerges at your side unannounced. You can't even speak in the pampa. I shouldn't even think about burying him! It's better to leave. After all, what difference does it make if he's eaten by birds or worms."

Once more he lifted the dead man's head, carefully this time, and gently closed his eyes, as if he were locking death inside that recumbent body. He climbed up the slope of the embankment with his bag over his shoulder and continued down the railroad tracks. Shortly before seven, he decided to spend the night right where he found himself. He settled down at the foot of the embankment. A little while later, the young man with the blond beard showed up. He looked at the sun and went down to where the old man was.

But yes, he'd had a good night looking after the young man with the blond beard! He wanted to stop his thoughts from spiraling and turn to the serene memory of the nighttime hours, when he watched over the blond man's sleep with that slightly awkward tenderness of the lonely. The young man slept beside him without even knowing that the old man was protecting him. But the old man was now doomed to think of another memory. Without being able to help it, he thought of a jail cell, of being put in a jail cell "for having murdered that poor wretch." It would be useless, swearing, pleading, screaming, begging, crying, useless. He would end up in a jail cell forever. Jail cells are always forever. Only he would know that he was incapable of killing anyone. Everyone else, the whole world, all the millions of people in the world, would think he was a murderer. "You need a witness to prove you haven't killed anyone." He thought he had only one way out: to follow one suicide with another.

It was already completely light out. He calmly accepted that his fate was sealed. But the night before (perhaps his last) he had had a good time while the man with the blond beard slept. He remembered having said, like the suicide before him, that one day they'd also find him dead by the side of the tracks. You never know when you're pronouncing your own death sentence.

He took off down the embankment and lay on the damp green grass. Without rushing, he rolled and lit a cigarette. The jigsaw puzzle being assembled inside his brain was supposed to give him some key to his own death. He noticed a question was haunting him: "What if the young man with the blond beard found me lying dead at the foot of the embankment, as I found the other one?" Once the question was put into words, he understood everything. "It won't happen. It can't happen. Because then there'd be no other escape for him. He'd have to follow me. As I followed the other. As the other had followed someone before him. And so on for who knows how long."

Certain he was changing the course of his destiny, he grabbed his bag and ran across the tracks. There he waited, hidden in some bushes on the northern slope. An hour later, in the distance, he saw the young man with the blond beard approaching along the southern tracks, and he said to himself, "There's no danger of the birds alerting him."

Like an animal he descended the slope, at the foot of which, lying face down, he made the sign of the cross with the tip of his knife, and, grasping it with both hands, carefully sunk it into his throat.

The Hunt

I

THE EARLY MORNING AIR was dry and cold after the snowfall. With his face pressed against the window, Marcos watched as the truck drove away. Slowly, the vehicle went down the street and around the corner to reach the road heading south.

The village continued prolonging the night as things began to regain their own colors surrounded by the transparent steel of the air. Yet, at that very moment, other hunters on other streets were warming up their car engines or starting to load blankets, tin cans, and boxes of ammunition just as his father, his brother Francisco, Martin (the lawyer), Hugo (the German), and Louis (the best hunter in town) had done a short while before.

By now the truck would be on the highway and the men would be making jokes, praising the good weather or recounting last night's dreams. Marcos knew the pent-up joy travelers feel getting on the road very early in the morning. With his face pressed against the glass, he tried to imagine the conversations the hunters would be having, as though he could recreate the hunt from the sofa where he was kneeling. The only reason he wasn't allowed to go that year was that he was still very young, because "it didn't make sense for him, at eleven years old, to spend five days in an uncomfortable cabin, getting up at dawn in the freezing cold, and climbing the hills with a heavy rifle."

With bitterness and shame, Marcos remembered his pleas and his father's reasons. His protests had been useless, and now, after seeing the men and his brother leave, he felt that every denied request was a seed of hatred inside his heart.

When his father kissed him before he climbed in the truck, a thought came to him that terrified him and for which he hardly felt responsible: a secret voice, similar to his own, told him that he wished his father would die. Only Francisco waved goodbye as he got in the truck. The father, however, did not turn around, as though there was nothing and no one behind him.

Bitterness is not easy to placate. The mother came into the living room and said, "Next year you'll all go." And luckily, it didn't occur to her to suggest that he go back to bed, because he wouldn't have been able to. The only one with any tact was the mother, who went to her room and left him alone. By now they would have reached the suburbs of the neighboring town, Marcos thought, but he couldn't be bothered to follow them in his mind.

Although he was sure he wouldn't be able to fall asleep, he climbed the stairs and went to his room. His bed was waiting for him next to Francisco's, on top of which, left behind, there lay an empty box of ammunition.

II

The only thing that surprised him (because even though he was only eleven years old, he knew as much as possible about hunting and weapons) was the exploding larches.

They wore red jackets so other hunters wouldn't mistake their movements for an animal's. When they got off the road and went deeper into the forest, they had to be extremely careful as they climbed because the ground was frozen. Finally, the boy worked up the courage to say, "It sounds like those shots are coming from our rifles." "What shots?" his father replied. For the first time in many weeks the boy saw him smile: his father had brought him along reluctantly, on the grounds that he was still too young. "Like this one," said the boy. The explosion had come from the same place where they were standing. "They're not shots," said the father. "They're larch trees bursting from the cold." The trees had cracks all along their trunks. Shells of snow imprisoned the branches.

They stopped next to a group of tall stones glittering in the sun. There they stood motionless for a couple of hours, almost always in silence, eyes and ears attentive, as if they were surrounded by darkness and menaced by a threatening presence. "The good hunter," said Louis, "must have patience and an iron will." Occasionally, the hunters were startled by the scurrying of some small rodent moving the branches. Your hands and feet become your enemies. The cold estranges them, and you have to make sure the blood flowing through them doesn't stand still.

Suddenly the boy felt himself shiver. The father raised his gun, and he did the same. It was too late. Something animal leapt, and about two hundred feet away, half hidden by the branches, a deer appeared. It stopped and sniffed. Only its head moved, which, from a distance, seemed mechanical. The father gently lowered his gun. "It's a doe," he whispered. The boy lowered his gun, too. The hunting of does was forbidden. "Be still," the father said almost voicelessly, "The buck might show up." They waited. But suddenly, as if impelled by a mechanical device, the animal was lost among the larches bursting from the cold.

At night the five men discussed the hunt. The boy listened. They cooked, drank, and talked about their guns as they cleaned them. Hugo, the German, vowed never to use his Winchester again because it pulled to the right. "We tried it when there wasn't any wind. Martin is my witness. As soon as I get back, I'm selling it."

It was almost night when Louis arrived at the cabin. He had gone out alone. Louis was a fairly quiet man, but he was so agitated when he came in that he took the floor and wouldn't let anyone else speak. He had met a pair of hunters who, like himself, swore they'd seen the tracks of an enormous stag. After last night's snowfall, the beast had wandered around the lake to the east on the shore opposite Marval's cabin. Unfortunately, a loathsome dog had done nothing but bark until they went to Marval's and got him locked away.

On the third night of the hunt, they were finally talking about something serious. Up to that point they had only caught small game, and almost for the sole pleasure of using and testing their guns. The fact that there was a large stag in the area lifted their spirits.

They drank more than ever, and Hugo announced he would be leaving very early, and taking with him something to eat. The others resigned themselves to the idea of not coming back for lunch the following day.

They climbed into their bunk beds and within ten minutes everyone except the boy was snoring. He coughed. His throat felt parched as supple deer leapt slowly across his forehead and through the gelatinous air. He started coughing again, but finally fell asleep. He was awakened by the smell of coffee. It was still pitch-black outside. The father approached him with an accusatory look. "You're staying in bed today. You've been coughing all night." He drank a cup of coffee and watched the men leave.

The cabin was small. It had six bunk beds, a large fireplace, and a long pine table with two matching benches.

He got dressed. His Winchester was next to the cabin's only door. He began reading the comics page he found in a crumpled-up newspaper. He warmed up more coffee and returned to his bunk, which was above his father's. It occurred to him that the others had been right: he was still too young to go hunting.

White and incredibly pure, the hill looked as if it had just risen from the earth. The snow-covered road winding around it revealed the five hunters' footprints. The sun began to illuminate the forest, where the tallest trees already shone with reddish light on the tops of their snowy crowns. The hill was beautiful with its trees that at times seemed to mock the snow with green or vibrantly golden leaves. Birches, larches, cedars, walnuts; the solemn quietism of hundreds of fantastic trees penetrated the cold air with their metallic but living vegetality.

Watching the sunrise from the window, the boy felt happy in that lonely cabin at the foot of the hill. The only thing that bothered him was that he hadn't behaved as he would have liked. His father was right when he said that he wasn't old enough for an adventure like this. The day before he had felt incredibly cold while he waited with Hugo. They were determined not to turn in without having bagged something good, and in the end, they had returned practically empty-handed.

While he gazed at the forest, he thought about how in a couple more years he'd be able to bear four or five hours of hunting, even if it was cold enough outside to split a rock. Not even next year would he insist on being taken hunting in the middle of the winter on a trip lasting so many days.

His guilt was bothering him more than his mild headache and the burning in his throat when, suddenly, there emerged an apparition that at first made him think his eyes were playing tricks on him. It left him petrified.

About a hundred yards away, next to a small pine tree whose long branches extended softly to the ground, the enormous stag, with its gigantic antlers, stood motionless. It seemed to be contemplating the cabin. The boy's blood froze. He wanted to think but he couldn't.

He crept toward Hugo's bunk. The window beside it was the only one ajar. He moved stealthily, as if the animal could see him or sniff him through the cabin walls. From there he could reach the Winchester. He had two bullets in his pants pocket. He loaded the gun and leaned the barrel against the window sill. He took aim, holding his breath.

The gunshot shattered the stillness of the forest, the hill, the morning. He had not yet released the trigger or let the air out of his chest when the deer's antlers made the snow accumulated on the branches of the pine tree come tumbling down.

He felt the cold steel against his cheek. The stag fell to its knees and, driving its antlers into the snow, buried its snout between its hooves as if it were its last refuge. The hunter was terrified. He put his gun down and left the cabin. He followed the bullet's trajectory with slow steps. When he reached the animal, he sat down beside it. It had sixteen points. It was still warm. It had a reddish coat and, next to the hole left by the bullet, there was a small triangle of white, swirly fur. The rest of its coat seemed to originate from this spot, spreading out from it in an orderly pattern. The stag had a wild smell, the smell of the forest, but it also smelled like blood, the red and black blood that traveled from the animal's entrails through the snow into the bowels of the earth.

Branch, stone, and bone: these three kingdoms seemed to combine in those beautiful antlers that now harbored the double cold of snow and death. Nights and sunrises, high noons, rains, and winds, streams and hills; all were entombed in the deer's body. The chill of death passed over it like a wave of forlorn oblivion. So much vanquished life pained every leaf, every branch, every tree of the vegetal world where it had been born, reigned, and succumbed: the deer's motionless body was like the forest's tomb.

The boy stroked the animal's back and its bent antlers. He stood up, buried his hands in his pockets, and returned to the cabin crying. He wouldn't have been able to say who was the hunter and who was the hunted.

From the cabin's window he now gazed through his tears at the hopeless stag that lay fallen at the foot of the hill. When, after hours that felt like centuries, the men appeared at the end of the road, the boy ran out to meet them. He caught up with them next to the deer.

They carried the hunter on their shoulders. The deer was dragged behind them. There was singing and alcohol. Even the boy drank a gulp of the sharp liquid that turned to flames inside his chest.

Instead of kissing him, the father extended his hand, and the boy stood there staring at him like a stranger. Then they gutted the animal and lay it open on the roof of the truck, with its antlers facing forward as though it were a figure-head. And they decided to return home because no one felt capable anymore of outdoing the game bagged by the boy.

Someone poured a copious stream of the liquor they were drinking into the fireplace and a sonorous flame burst out among the ash-covered embers. They tied the deer down with ropes and made their departure. Countless times on the ride home the boy had to tell the story of how'd he shot the deer. No less than fifty men, over several days, had searched for the deer's tracks and dreamed of sighting it. But he, a boy, had been the fortunate one. And all thanks to the cough which had kept him in the cabin. It was incredible luck and the guarantee of a great hunter's destiny. A man can spend years, his entire life, searching for game like that and die without ever finding it.

The truck advanced slowly to prolong the victory. The other hunters cheered them as they passed. They entered the village at dusk, as a bitter cold set in.

III

As if he were talking to himself, Marcos said, "If they left after lunch and the road is clear, they'll get here in half an hour." The mother said, "Next year you'll all go," as if she too were alone.

There was a long silence. Marcos liked being with the mother while she sewed. "Maybe they'll bring him," said Marcos. "Who?" the mother asked without lifting her head. "The deer," Marcos answered. "What deer?" said the mother uneasily as she looked up and lowered her sewing. The boy didn't answer. He went to the sofa to kneel and lean his forehead against the window.

After the mother left, Marcos reached for the switch of the only lamp that was lit. The star-filled night surrounded the house and gathered it up like an immense bejeweled hand. A light that barely moved appeared between the hedges. "It's the truck," said the boy to himself. The noise of the engine disrupted the night. The truck stopped in front of the house and Marcos lifted his hands to his eyes, his mouth, his heart.

Joylessly, the men and Francisco got out of the truck. The mother came down from her room. Their neighbors came out into the street. They congratulated the hunters. The father and Francisco entered the house. Friends and neighbors followed them inside. Marcos turned on the light. There was coffee waiting for them. The father finally spoke: "It was very strange. We were coming down the hill today and, about a hundred yards from the cabin . . ."

Marcos slipped down a hallway and closed a door behind him. He had a dark feeling. He didn't want to hear anything because, hazily, he realized that at that moment his innocence was at risk.

Aromatic Herbs

A DREAM VISITS ME from time to time like a recurring fever. Each version differs slightly from the last. Sometimes
the woman's scarf is made of silk or wool or a very delicate
gauze, but it's always black and white, and very long, with
wavy stripes, and very docile to the wind.

A man arrives by plane after a short flight and walks
towards the roundabout in front of the airport in Sainte
Ercienne. Often, I have no idea who the traveler is; often,
as is typical in dreams, I know and I don't know, and even
without knowing who he is, I have no doubt that he's me.
Next to the roundabout, where there are three or four
small trees and beds of aromatic herbs like in the well-
manicured gardens of a medieval cloister, Eleonora, with a
convertible beside her, is standing waiting for me, wrapped
in her scarf.

We hardly speak. Then we drive along a hilly path where
one can see the rust-colored crowns of the chestnut trees.
Gusts of wind send Eleonora's scarf floating in the air. This
happens several times, until finally the scarf catches in one of
the wheels, and Eleonora is torn violently from her seat, and
I with her. We crash into the side of the hill, and I notice that
my blood stains her lifeless face.

Curiously, the model of the car varies. Eleonora, whom I've only met in dreams, is usually dressed in different ways but she always wears the scarf. One time I caught the vaguest glimpse of the house that awaits us and at which we never arrive: it has vast stone terraces and overlooks an ocher-colored vineyard. Little by little I have been falling in love with Eleonora. That she doesn't actually exist used to terrify me. Since then, I've learned that dreams are made of a substance no less consistent, true, or concrete than our mellifluous everyday reality. What's more, perhaps there's a parallel hell where we'll pay for the sins we commit in our dreams. And, conversely, a paradise.

That love leads us to death, time and time again, hardly matters. From the moment I get off the plane, I see her standing there, calmly waiting for me. A happy silence affords us a secret, seemingly timeless form of love. We never know we're going to die, or maybe we do, we know but we don't say it, because only in silence can we recall the names of the aromatic plants that fill the roundabout in Sainte Ercienne, and, after having listed them and evoked their scents, we die again.

When anguished by the idea that Eleonora's existence depended on my dreams, I would cling with innocent and delirious hope to the possibility that I was the one being dreamed of, that I was the one who only existed when Eleonora revived me in a recurring dream that visited her from time to time.

My business partner insists that it's in our interest to purchase the harvest of a small winery in Sainte Ercienne. I'm against it. What's more, I believe my opposition has something to do with my not wanting to travel in one of those small, beat-up airplanes that are practically the only way to reach the area.

After these repeated deaths, all that remains is for a new dream to rescue us from this well of absence that is the days themselves, and then we can meet again at the roundabout in front of the Sainte Ercienne airport, so that after patiently evoking the colors, shapes, and smells of each of the aromatic herbs, we find again that circular destiny in which each of our deaths is secretly linked to one of those innocent or malevolent plants, each named with a different name, each with its own perfume.

The behavior of many couples in literature shouldn't be freed from responsibility for this habit my dream has become. On the other hand, the compulsory deaths of Romeo and Juliet— to cite one such case—and their compulsory resurrection at each rereading or performance is not without mystery, a fact that not so vaguely suggests that literary works are also circular.

A shock of rust runs over the tops of the chestnut trees. Eleonora's hair was also rust-colored, and I lightly grazed it with my hand resting on the back of her seat. The open sky above us was a very pale blue and the silence between us made the sounds of the engine, the wind, the brakes on the hilly path's sharp curves even more present, especially the sound of the wind that, at times, suddenly snatched Eleonora's woolen scarf and made it flutter with its wavy black and white stripes in the fresh morning air.

And once again a violent gust of wind grabs the scarf, which gets entangled in the spokes of a rear wheel, and Eleonora is dragged backwards, and the car seems to want to climb the hillside in the wake of a din of metal and glass thrown against stone, and I notice my blood is cooling on Eleonora's face.

Because she'd come to pick me up at Sainte Ercienne's small airport, where a roundabout full of aromatic herbs such as sage, rue, apple mint, thyme, rosemary, and oregano perfumed the country air of that village erected on a modest open plain between the hills.

And that's how I ended up in Eleonora's car after the short flight from Lyon to Sainte Ercienne, looking at the swift and tawny roofs of the chestnut trees behind her motionless, rust-colored hair, while I listed in my head the names of the aromatic herbs.

And now it's back to waiting. Waiting for the stars to align so I can fly from Lyon to Eleonora's hills. To arrive at the roundabout planted with ginger and mallow, broad-leaved lavender and saffron. To meet once again and travel together along the undulating and serpentine road until the wind snatches away that long strip of black-and-white silk, and when it becomes entangled in the spokes of the rear wheel, we crash against the hillside, and my blood covers Eleonora's face, and we die again, and I say: once again I'll have to wait until I can return to die forever evoking the names of pennyroyal and lavender in that cool autumn morning that every now and then becomes once again the final morning.

On an ocher-colored morning of trees and golden sunshine, the six or seven passengers who had just arrived from Lyon to the small southern village of Sainte Ercienne descended from an airplane. They went their separate ways without saying goodbye, as if minutes before they hadn't shared, along with their common destination, the secret terror and incomprehensible euphoria of the air.

One of the passengers walks resolutely toward a roundabout filled with small plants, where a woman is waiting for him next to a car. A long black-and-white scarf the wind sends floating in the air accentuates the woman's stillness.

Now they are driving along a corniche and the wind seems to attack the car at different points as they round the hill. The air is cool but it is the scarf more than the cold that signals the changes in the wind's direction. And when the sun shines straight on the characters' faces (the man is me, and the woman, Eleonora) the scarf flees like a bird from around Eleonora's neck and flies backwards. (Hazily, I remember a certain obligation regarding a winery.)

Suddenly, at the top of the hill, I looked down at the golden tops of the chestnut trees that barely reached the height of the road. The scarf changed direction violently and fell like lead to the pavement. I saw Eleonora straighten and turn her face toward me with a brief, imploring glance. She let go of the steering wheel and the car seemed to pick up speed. We embraced each other almost mid-air, when we had already crashed into the hillside and the crowns of the chestnut trees were overturned and my blood stained the taut scarf caught in the back wheel of the car, and her face cooled under mine, and we were entering a place nocturnal and brilliant, forgotten by the autumn sun forever, forever.

But our death is always different, or rather, it always has a different name. It goes like this: as we drive, we list the names of the aromatic herbs in our heads. The names of other spices get mixed in with those of the aromatics: bay leaf and basil, clove and oregano. I think the roundabout also has lavender and mallow, a nutmeg and a camphor tree. Naturally, the order in which we evoke them varies. I think the crash occurs when we finish naming all the plants in the roundabout. The last one—it always changes—pronounces our death.

My business partner is right. He's found a buyer for the harvest before we've even purchased it. The offer stands until the end of the month, so on Thursday I'll travel to Sainte Ercienne to finalize the deal.

And the man arrives with the group and separates from it. Alone, he walks toward a roundabout filled with shrubs, maybe aromatic herbs. There's a spectator who narrates these events like in a movie. As one part of him follows what's happening, the other enumerates: marjoram, mistol, thyme, myrtus, salvia. The man heads toward that bundle of confused aromas and between branches that are neither ginger nor mallow, nor rue nor anise, but chestnut, he spots the woman who came to wait for him. She's standing beside a car. He notices that the wind blows unevenly, in fleeting gusts, because the scarf of heavy black-and-white cloth at times floats and moves away from her body, and then falls at her feet, stops, and flutters again.

The traveler approaches her and his stride is as energetic as before, but now the air seems like a translucent syrup, an invisible jelly that slows his gait as if time has stretched elastically, and suddenly there are many more instants within the same space, so that traveling a distance has become a hardly perceptible movement.

The woman is still. Only the scarf tends to rise, float, and then fall, surely with an audible sound. And they look at each other from across a distance that barely shrinks despite the man's steps and their anxiousness to meet, which subtly appears in the sparkle in their eyes, their secret breaths, their pulses, which no one can register but me, as I contemplate the meeting and say the names of wormwood and myrtle, oregano and vanilla, detecting the rising flush of their cheeks and their accelerating pulses, and a growing heat within their breasts, and a sudden emptiness in their bellies, and a very vague and shallow trembling of their lips.

They're face-to-face now, and I see, though I do not hear, that very few words pass between them, and they get in the car, which smells of leather even though its top is down under the pale-blue autumn sky. She drives down a long road. I see them from the front, from behind, from the side, from above. She is attentive to the road. He, to the scarf, which has twice already freed itself violently like the tail of a comet, before returning to a quiet stillness.

Finally, and in order to relax, I realize I'm the man, the woman is Eleonora, the approaching hills over which we'll have to climb are her native ones, the ones she has spoken to me of so many times, and then, peacefully, I once again name the spices, the aromatic herbs: broad-leaved lavender, wormwood, rosemary, cinnamon, cumin, ginger . . . and mustard and myrtle? Are they there?

Are they aromatic herbs? Was there thyme and verbena, pennyroyal and anise?

Once again, the scarf flees like a terrified animal. Once again Eleonora collects it. The air is cool, but its chill is more noticeable from the scarf that moves in the wind than from the dry transparency that eagerly rummages through the roots of her hair—and travels across her skin with its crystalline smoothness. And it's that the wind is round in the hills: here, when we ascend, we leave the sun behind us and the wind disappears. We circle the top of the hill and begin to descend, and the sun is in front of us, and with it the wind returns, searching for the black-and-white scarf until it overtakes it, and pulls it back, and then we start climbing again and the air calms, and I see Eleonora's face in profile against the crowns of the chestnut trees planted on the slope, lower than the road, which have the generosity, from time to time, to frame her profile against the incredibly distant pale-blue sky.

But who has died here? Me? Certainly. Or is it just a way to end the trip, and therefore no one has died, but no one can go on ascending and descending the hills anymore? Or is it all finished, Eleonora, me, the trip? Or do we have to list the herbs again and start all over? And yet another question: Are English lavender, fringed lavender, and lavender all the same thing, do they all have the same perfume, and are they all the color of Eleonora's eyes when autumn shines on the hills of Sainte Ercienne? And yet another question: Could it be that this is my heaven, or my hell, and I'll repeat my dream forever and ever, like a blessing or a curse?

Enemies

I WRAP MYSELF in a sheet (just like she did a moment ago) and go looking for her. She's in the living room. I stop and take cover behind an armchair, which shields me from the waist down. Vailda (I think that's her name) inevitably reminds me of one of those Greek and Roman figures etched in Malet's history books. I can't tell her this. You can hardly tell women anything. For example: before I'd even spoken to her, they told me she was from one of those northern countries. I hadn't asked. Among other reasons, because I don't care. Basically, the only thing I care about is looking at her. She's full of a distinct energy, and learning more about her doesn't help you figure it out. A few minutes ago, when we were in the other room, she sat up in bed. We'd just woken up. She looked at me (sometimes her eyes are quite vacant), fixed her hair, wrapped herself in a sheet, and slid silently toward the door. There, without a moment's pause, she announced she was going to make some tea and disappeared. At least she wore the sheet. Standing naked, she's almost intolerable. There are degrees of nudity. In any case, Vailda is more naked than any other being I've ever seen without clothes on. More naked than an animal. After a while, since I don't hear any noise, I call out to her. Of course, she doesn't answer.

This is to be expected. Being and not being at the same time is part of her style. She hides herself even in her nakedness, and makes herself felt with a delirious intensity. And so, since she doesn't answer, I wrap myself in a sheet and go looking for her. And that's how I end up staring at her, trying in vain not to think about the etchings in Malet's history books.

I hadn't come to the sea to relax or enjoy myself. Rather, I came in search of that predictable peace that coastal cities offer in spring. I needed to work and my task required a particular type of tranquility I could only find by distancing myself from permanent things. I must say, I worked hard and the results were positive. What's more, I was happy with the silence, with the long, tense, almost cloister-like hours I kept during the first ten days. In the morning, I walked along the beach or the promenade, and in the afternoon, I worked. I'd go out to eat alone. Then I'd come back, read for a while, and sleep. I truly felt I was making good use of my time. I carefully guarded my solitude and silence, as you do with things that are delicate and vulnerable. Then one day, while I was at a restaurant, I spotted an old friend. Then I saw him again standing next to a cigarette shop. Quickly turning my head and picking up my pace spared me from having to talk with him and give useless explanations. On Thursday, however, I could not avoid him. He was as happy to see me as I was unhappy to see him. It was rather pathetic and I could barely hide my misery. I didn't tell him anything, of course. I had to employ one of those looks that demand complicity without meaning anything concrete. "Do you have a lady friend?" he asked, clumsily. I couldn't lie to him, but on the other hand, I didn't want to admit he was right about anything. "No, no lady friends," I replied. He invited me over to his house for dinner. I declined. He insisted. I wanted to run away. Out of laziness, I acquiesced.

Spend ten days alone and you can forget how to talk. I felt like a miserable wretch at dinner. I don't know why my friend thought I'd be enchanted by a certain young lady there. He assigned me to her, but I grew bored and, of course, so did she. After we had eaten, the young blonde whose name I think is Vailda arrived. She was assigned to someone else. We spoiled our host's plan by choosing each other. Having hardly spoken, we chose each other with the apparent serenity of very violent things. A little while later we were walking down a backstreet leading to the port. We went to have a cup of wine in a tavern that had become famous a few years ago precisely because they served Moselle by the cup. Afterward we slept at my place. Of course, she moved in. Goodbye silence. Goodbye work. Goodbye loneliness.

I look at this beautiful woman, and Vailda (I think that's her name) is truly beautiful, there's no need for other adjectives, it has nothing to do with what I or anyone else considers beautiful; she's beautiful, moreover, for everyone; not like a straight line or an animal that's very healthy and very young; what I mean is: not only is she beautiful like things that are indisputably beautiful, she is beautiful the way a symbol is. Well, as I was saying, I look at this woman and think about merging with her again, and it's as though our natures were completely contrary, as though I were from another planet, and the only way I can experience being human is by passing through her body. With my humanity at stake, I feel like my entire being is oriented toward Vailda and my

hands reach out for that which is now the entire human species. And now I can even hear life inside her, a different life,
and, believe me, I seem to hear the hum of the constellations.
You have to understand, it is impossible not to love a woman
like Vailda. Then I fall asleep in her hair. When I opened
my eyes it all came back to me (her smell, her heartbeat,
her breath) and my mouth watered. She was already awake.
Without opening her eyes, she told me she had a revolver in
her purse. I wrapped myself in my sheet (or hers). I went to
the other room. I took out the revolver. It was already dark.
I came back. I kissed her. I stepped out onto the terrace.
The sound of the sea was everywhere. I looked around at
the sky, the black water moved by the light of the stars, the
ash-colored foam on the beach. I fired all six shots into the
sea because I knew they wouldn't hit anything. The Southern
Cross pulsed in the firmament like an eternal animal. Vailda
screamed at me, insulted me, cursed me. Anger transformed
her into a vociferous beast. I didn't look at her, but I could
imagine what her beautiful face looked like when she was
upset, her body writhing with furious impotence. Without
turning around, still wrapped in a sheet, I asked her to leave. I
waited with my face turned toward the night of sea and stars.
I heard her pace around barefoot. She went into the other
room. I heard the zipper of her purse a couple of times. Then
her footsteps again, but now she was wearing shoes. My back
was still turned. She opened the door. The Southern Cross
was still reclining in the shadows. She slammed the door shut.

I went back to the living room and this is how I saw myself: alone, with a sheet for clothing, and an empty revolver
in my hand. I felt ridiculous. I tried not to hear myself think.

I poured myself a small glass of red wine left over from lunch, drank it, and went to lie down. I woke up two hours ago. In the apartment, on my skin, there is still a vague scent of love and sulfur, which slowly dissipates.

Figs and Jasmines

DEATH USED TO BE DIFFERENT. Something has changed in the way we think about death or the way we die. It's not that I've changed. Maybe it's just time, pure time, that makes us see the same things as if they were different. Buenos Aires used to be a city of boys with erector sets, it was a city of ladies who played the violin, children witnessed masked carnivals, and every neighborhood had blacksmiths because the city and the countryside were more blended together. The bakers, the milkmen, the wicker peddlers, the trash collectors; everyone had horse-drawn carts. Even the dead were carried away in shiny hearses led by shiny-hooved horses. On summer afternoons, for example, after we'd taken our baths, we'd go out in the street and play with our friends. Races around the block and games of rango y mida, cops and robbers, and tipcat were organized on street corners. When the first shadows began to slip over the tops of the plátano trees, our aunts and grandmas would call us in to eat. Later, the lucky ones would take a trip to the ice cream parlor four blocks away for a second dessert. They would eat chocolate ice cream sandwiches with wafers bearing familiar phrases like, "Farewell, pretty gal" or "That's my cup of tea." It was the age of wisteria, of coleus, of pinstripe pants and thick denim, the age of white berets and red berets. We'd smoke sarsaparilla. Some men wore garters on their shirt sleeves and chatelaines; everyone wore straw hats in the summer and high boots year round. We would hurt each other's feelings by calling each other saps, and if you had a big head, your nickname was Zeppelin. Back then, dying was romantic. Not just anyone died. Those who died were very old and very young. Unlike now, when anyone can die. My house had a fig tree. I don't know if the fig tree held any prestige. I don't even remember us talking about it, but it was the most important part of the house. And not just because it was in the middle of the courtyard, or because its generous branches spread over our roofs and those of our neighbors. It was important in a way that was somewhat secret and profound. In a home, certain objects will take on a special value for no apparent reason. In my home it was the fig tree. Our fig tree bore white figs, not black ones. To me, white figs are more dignified than black ones. As a child, when I'd visit a home with a tree that grew black figs, I'd feel an overwhelming certainty that the people who lived there were our inferiors. Our home also had numerous jasmines. I've always found jasmines to be sickeningly sweet. They give me the same bad feeling in the back of my palate that one gets after eating too much dulce de leche. But it's a pleasure to remember those jasmines from my childhood. They were probably the same as all the other jasmines, but to me there was something special about them. I'm talking about those jasmines with fleshy white petals, the ones that turn brown in the place where their petals break off. It's a pleasure remembering the fig tree and how the wind would fill with its vegetal aroma as it passed sonorously through its branches. And it's a pleasure to remember those figs and the sticky milk they released when they were plucked before their time. Those figs seemed to stick to the hands of anyone who wouldn't let them ripen. My grandmas and aunts wouldn't let me eat more than four or five figs at a time because otherwise I'd get sores in the corners of my mouth. As for the jasmines, their intoxicating scent filled the house, imposing a certain tone of voice on summer nights—I wasn't allowed to go out to play until after I'd taken my bath and watered them. I hated that chore, and yet I carried a certain attachment to those jasmines because of things I knew about them that I now prefer to remember hazily. The figs and jasmines of my childhood, that time when dying was a little bit magical and a little bit sordid, and, at the same time, something one had no right to do. Yet, impossible as it may seem, dying held a certain appeal. It was like securing a sort of glory or family sainthood. Those who died were always being talked about or alluded to. Secretly, they continued to rule the lives of the living. I'm going to say something foolish: people could kill themselves out of sheer egomania because in the end they'd wind up more relevant dead than alive. I remember my childhood filled with the smell of Faber No. 2 pencils, the smell of jasmine, the soft sound of the wind moving the branches of the fig tree. I remember how the jasmines would brown where their petals had broken off, and how your hands would get sticky from touching the fig tree's milky stems, and I insist that to die back then was to fill a house, a neighborhood, a city, the world. But those who died were guilty. It was as if they'd snapped a petal off one of the jasmines or plucked a fig

before it had ripened. They were the embodiment of betrayal. Needless betrayal. I felt they were guilty of mixing
love with hate. To be precise: it was at that time I began to
feel disgust for the dead. Hate, shame, resentment, but especially disgust. I'd also had the chance to die. Mine was with
the measles. My fever wouldn't go down. I noticed a circle of
terrified and anguished people had formed around me. The
doctor stayed by my side all night long giving orders that were
fearfully obeyed. I was sure sinister things would happen if I
decided to die. Aside from the flowers and the weeping and
my school friends and the neighbors and people visiting and
mourning and a hundred other predictable scenes, the same
thing would end up happening to me: they'd turn me into
a family saint, a household hero for having died. They'd set
up an altar with my picture and some little candles and the
silver metal vase. And in November, they'd fill the vase with
dahlias from the garden. The same thing would happen: "If
he were alive, he'd say . . ." Everything that occurred after my
death would be determined by my absence. And so, I chose
to live, not so much because I wanted to go on living, but
because dying disgusted me. You don't understand anything
when you're a kid. And sometimes, when I was eating a fig
and watering the jasmines, I'd think it was better to play the
fool and simply let the days go idly by.

By the Word

WHEN HE FELL, he rolled like a drunk in a movie, violently tossed from a dark tavern. Half-stunned, half-incredulous, he took a second to accept that he'd heard one last phrase spoken in an absurdly biblical and threatening tone.

His cap, which someone had pulled down to his nose with a humiliating tug on the brim, still blinded him. "Perfect," he thought, until he was interrupted by a hiccup. "Perfect. This is the perfect opportunity to take a nap." And making the most of the push, the tug, and the kick, he fell asleep.

He couldn't have looked any more destitute. An ordinary pair of black pants, stained and frayed, covered his legs, which were open at an angle of defeat. His lean arms and torso, though visibly firm, seemed to have begun deteriorating due to poverty and neglect rather than age. A shirt made of coarse gray fabric clung to his neck. His face, in profile, was all wrinkled skin and a graying beard. Then there was the cap, ridiculously pulled down to his eyes, and, underneath it, his docile, fallen hair, hair that could harbor madness or prophecy.

He slept on his chest with his arms and legs splayed. The air left his mouth desperately as if trying to escape from hell. And it was the longing and vehemence of his breath that told you the sleeping man was wrought by rigor and passion.

Suddenly he's awake. He turns onto his back, brings his feet together, and raises his arms above his head. Stretched out on the floor he resembles a diver in midair. He relaxes his muscles and snaps off his cap, exposing his high forehead and wild gray hair. He jumps to his feet. He extends his arms like a blind man. He rubs his eyes. His hands are agitated and incredulous as they pass over his cheeks. He walks over to one of the cell walls. He rests his palms against the cold metal and strokes the smooth, polished surface.

The cube must be about ten feet each way. There are no doors or windows, no cracks through which a single drop of light or air could filter. There's no furniture, not even a lamp. No dust, either. The dim light by which he sees must somehow be trapped in there with him.

He purses his lips and emits a timid and ridiculous little test whistle. It comes out perfectly normal, as though he were whistling in any old room. Without dropping his cap, he walks over to one of the cube's corners and takes a seat on the floor.

With a trace of curiosity, he tried to figure out how he got there. He thought back to the last time he remembered himself free. "I left home at five. I walked across the park. I ran into Tobias. We joked about the piles of branches the kids had made to burn on Saint John's Eve. I crossed the intersection diagonally. I went into a bar and ordered a gin. I sat down at a table where people were playing cards. After that, I don't remember anything."

Suddenly he felt a surge of rage. A kind of smoldering tirade rose from his chest. He started pacing the cube, his hands trembling, his ears flattened back like an alert animal's.

"It's useless," he thought, "this cube is useless. It won't accomplish anything; it won't get anything out of me. It's terrible because it's useless."

He'd tortured himself thousands of times by imagining that he was locked in a narrow closet or the trunk of a car or a submarine. But now that his recurring nightmare was real, he didn't feel the horrible tightness he'd imagined. From the very start, what fed his anxiety was the gratuitousness of it all, the absurdity and unnaturalness of his situation.

He returned to his corner as if compelled by some dark instinct to repeat what limited actions were available to him. But he was too conscious of his every movement, and he realized choosing that corner was an act of freedom. He wanted to exercise the freedom that destiny had denied him. He thought, however, and not without distaste, that he might not be in the same corner as before. It was impossible to differentiate between anything inside the cube.

Disregarding memory, habit, and sanity, he could imagine himself shrunken like an insect inside a small metal box. Or he was a monstrous giant enclosed in a cube whose walls measured an acre each. Without a frame of reference, space dissolves into the curves of time; centuries pass in an instant, and instants last a century. As long as he remained proportional to the cube, his actual size could have been modified with dreamlike perversity. But without abandoning his unstoppable irony, he restrained his delirious imagination and said to himself: "I could calculate the dimensions of the cube. I'm six feet tall. I could make a strip out of my clothing that's exactly my height. Then I could measure one side of the cube by dividing the strip proportionally until I arrived at a unit that was, in turn, proportional to the dimension of a side. Knowing the length of one side, I could figure out the diagonals. All I would need to do is square the length of the side, multiply that result by two, and then find the square root of the total. I could give the cube a name and furnish it in my mind. I could imagine the pictures I'd hang on the walls and paint it, give it life, a window here, a bookshelf there. I could fill it with books written in my mind. I could live here for centuries by searching inside my heart. I could invent new fashions, design political structures, develop a philosophy, and lay the groundwork for a new pedagogy. I could pray. I could infuse every word of every prayer with vim and vigor, and revive in me that deadened and dry deposit of religious faith whose absence I do not regret and whose presence I do not miss."

Something hidden but very much alive told him that if he yielded even imperceptibly, he'd once again be able to go in and out of his home, to cross the park at any hour, to have a drink at the bar whenever, to continue earning his bread and modest glasses of gin from his trade making carpenters' benches. But he also knew that to give in would be to misuse his life. In a way that was even more obscure and hidden, but more real than the hilt of a knife, he understood that freedom was a virtue that he had practiced with the normalcy and urgency with which he breathed. Only at that moment, however, did the certainty that it was a virtue reveal itself to him so clearly. It was a matter of maintaining it or relinquishing it. That was all. But he didn't think of it as a problem; or, at any rate, he already knew the solution. He realized that he would make no effort to disguise the truth. He would not invent burdensome systems or construct ornate windows in the cube. He was there, and it was necessary to stick to that reality.

Hazily, he imagined himself without arms and legs. He looked at his battered cap. He unfastened the clasp and fastened it again. Then he looked at his hands, his arms, his feet. He looked at himself as if he were a stranger, and not without some charity. "I could try to sleep for a bit," he said to himself, "but sleeping would also be useless. The cube is the cube, and I am me."

For a while he sat there thinking, stretching the corners of his mouth with his thumb and his forefinger. "The cube is the cube, and I am me," he said aloud this time, but he barely managed to finish his sentence. Something moved on the ceiling in the opposite corner, diagonal to the one he was sitting in. He walked slowly to the other end of the cube to get a closer look. The corner, which until a moment ago had been perfectly normal, had developed a growth. "What is that!" he cried out in horror. And as he uttered those words, new forms, like monstrous, watery branches, suddenly grew from the ceiling and stood rigid as stalactites. Disgusted, he uttered a phrase expressing his contempt, and the forms multiplied capriciously.

He returned to his corner. He now had one leg tucked under him and the other extended along the floor. His elbow supported the weight of his body. Reclining like this with his cap in his hand, he spent a long time thinking. The forms remained motionless, without growing, without changing. He watched them attentively, with repulsion and disdain. He let out another whistle without taking his eyes off them, but nothing in the cube changed.

It took him a while to make the connection. More precisely: he did not want to be convinced. But after staring raptly for a long time at these abominable forms, suddenly, like someone not wanting to delay news of a tragedy, he shouted a word. He just wanted to prove what he already knew. A new form descended, like melting metal, and suddenly froze. He repeated the word, and new protrusions sprouted, and then, standing up and threatening them with his cap, he cursed them as if they were living beings, as if they were his enemies. Some of these repulsive forms now reached the floor, while others sprang up from the ground in abject profusion.

These atrocious growths were now sprouting from two corners of the cube. There was something vegetal about them, but also something animal and clumsy, and they grew in a dense, impenetrable thicket. He wasn't looking at them anymore. He had his head tucked between his knees and he was hugging himself in a fetal position. He imagined himself in a new womb, maturing for a new life. He lifted his head and, looking at the metallic branches, spoke again. "If only I could pray," he said. And more forms were born.

From now on, he thought, he would only say the words that formed the base of his memory, no matter how trivial or arbitrary they may have seemed before a possible witness. He remembered that his grandmother, in the house where he was born, had a garden with aromatic herbs. She claimed that, despite conventional wisdom, oregano, marjoram, and sandalwood were slightly different plants. And he spoke the three names of the bitter herbs whose old scents he could evoke and recover even now as he watched these piercing forms drip from the ceiling and grow from the floor.

And then he remembered a name that he'd always held onto as if shrouded in a mist of bashful forgetfulness, and he said it, and repeated it several times until his eyes closed from exhaustion.

And he remembered a corner of his city, in summer, also long ago, where there was a house with a gate covered in jasmine, and he spoke the names of the two streets where the house was located.

He said a friend's name. He said "carpenter's bench" because those were what he built for a living. He said "blue eyes" for reasons that were secret. He said the words "horse," "caress," "water," "friend," "ocean," "wine," "early," and "silence," because they were words he loved. He said "hammer" and "saw," "chisel" and "vise," "plane" and "jig" because they were the names of the tools of his trade, names that he never spoke aloud when he was alone working, but that he'd used every day.

Now the growths reached his feet and surrounded him. He pressed himself tightly against two walls and stood almost on tiptoes with his cap in his hand, glued to the last free corner of the cube.

Now the thicket left only a void in the shape of his body. He hadn't let go of his cap, which was flattened against the wall along with the back of his hand. The other hand, also open, rested against the other wall. He felt taller. He couldn't help feeling it was all nonsense, a diabolical and futile game, and not because he wasn't sure what was happening, but because he felt the world inside his heart in a way that was more lucid, more his own, and more secure than ever before.

Almost lazily he spoke the name of a memory again, as if memories had names. Two of the growths embedded themselves in him. One went through his hand and cap, the other through his foot. He shut his eyes and started to cry. The blood warmed his wounds like distant smoke.

"If only I could pray," he said again, faintly, and his other hand and foot were pierced. He felt his blood trickle down his fingers. And then, opening his eyes against the thicket already touching his face, he began to scream the final word, but he could not finish it: one last form sought his heart like a knife.

The Martyr

HERE, ABOUT THREE HUNDRED FEET from the point on the planet where the 34th parallel south and the 38th meridian west intersect, on the thirtieth floor of the Pampa Building located on the waterfront of the city of Buenos Aires, there are no flies.

Asleep in the folds of a cabbage or terrified on a delivery man's shoulder, they rarely reach these godforsaken heights.

All afternoon I've wandered from one side of my apartment to the other, and since it's spring you can't even hear the hiss of the heat passing through the radiators. No flies, no heat. My neighbors seem to have abandoned the building. The silence and the solitude have done away with time. (Malena was the last woman to visit my apartment. She was blonde and, aware of the impunity that being up so high granted her, walked around naked and recited Shakespeare and Darío, deliberately repeating the schoolgirl intonation her teachers had taught her as a child.)

Nothing. As I was saying, a planetary silence grows from the pit of the night to the exploding pulp of stars. I went to the kitchen for ice so I could pour myself a whiskey. Roigt was there sleeping. His snout against the tiles, his bitter smell, his short hair, his bulging eyes, his mutilated ears: how thankful I was for his passive, animal presence, silent yet vital. (I remember the day Malena brought him over. When she walked in, she looked at me with her slightly intoxicated eyes and announced she had a gift for me. When I saw the box full of holes I thought unhappily of a bird and how I needed to release it immediately. She took the lid off the box and the puppy rested its cold black nose on one of the edges. A minute later Roigt was skating across the waxed floors and making a detailed survey of his new home while Malena, shouting and laughing, told me five things at once, named ten people, drew open the curtains, and put on music.)

Sometimes I think living alone and almost never seeing people has changed me. Maybe Roigt is changed, too. (She named him that. Two years ago, she needed to have an operation. For two endless days, Malena skirted the edge of death. All her joie de vivre seemed to dissolve in pools of delirium and fever. Being by her side was like staring into an abyss. Once in a while, a glimmer of lucidity seemed to cool her burning forehead. I don't think I've ever been so afraid. In those anguished days, the importance of every moment became clear to me. I evoked the image of Malena while we listened to music, the two of us at peace, serenely, with that peace you find at the beach or in the countryside. Anyway. We made it through that and she insisted on talking about her experience. She told me that when she was certain she was going to die, she couldn't stop thinking of the word "Roigt." Roigt? Yes, Roigt. Did she know anyone by that name? No. Had she read that name in a book? Never. Roigt became a ladder, a way out, a hope, an aid. And holding on to that word, she reached a point where it didn't matter to her that she was going to die. Her skin had just walked through death; her pale-blue eyes were back from glimpsing eternity.)

So Roigt was in the kitchen, and he was now the only proof I had that the world was still the world. I took out some ice cubes and returned to the living room. I stepped out onto the balcony; yes, the stars were shining as always, but the streets were deserted, hardened, and pointlessly illuminated.

The breakup with Malena was horrible. It was a relief. It was agony. It was a chance to take a breath. I made concessions. So did she. We took a trip to Salta. We went to the south. We returned to our lives in Buenos Aires, to having too many friends and not enough solitude. We broke up. Malena is gone and I have my peace. That's what's important. I just called her on the phone. Not to talk with her or to hear her voice. I just wanted to make sure she's alive. She didn't pick up. The phone rang thirty-seven times. She's not home. I return to the balcony. Not even a car. No signs of life. Just Roigt and me. Roigt and me alone.

People aren't identical to their bodies. There's always a slight difference between a person and how they appear to us when we meet, like books with transparent pages where the lines don't match up. The information we get from a person when we see them for the first time is basically worthless because it's produced by our so-called objectivity, and our experience always distorts things. And on top of that, there are always those internal wrinkles, like poorly applied stickers whose colors end up running. Describing people belongs to the oral genre and happens almost exclusively between people who know each other very well. You can only describe someone effectively by virtue of the connivance that all intimacy presupposes. You need to share a certain sense of humor and agree upon the nuances of certain words and be able to draw upon common experiences or memories.

For example, if I say, "Malena isn't very tall," I'm telling a half truth because, even though she isn't tall, she seems to be. And the following sentence would tell you almost nothing about a woman: "She's rooted in the world with a certain frivolity, but, at the same time, a vague atmosphere of drama surrounds her."

Sometimes she falls into brief, yet loaded, silences. Peace is something Malena never knows. A comment or a sudden laugh forms in her mouth and mutilates the silence. (I have often imagined her alone, in her room, lying in bed, gently crying with only her eyes, until self-consciousness forces her to proceed with dignity cloaked in humor, and then she gets up, goes to the liquor cabinet, pours herself a whiskey, and puts on some music before "fixing her face." In these scenarios Malena is wearing yellow pants.)

Her presence is always invigorating and positive. Her hands are very economical and passive, and often they seem to forget where they are. I think Malena thinks her hands are ugly and that's what keeps them quiet. You'll almost never see a hand of hers swoop like a bird to her hair or land in a fold of her dress. Her hands straighten, arrange, and return unnoticed, unnoticed because when she makes those movements, she uses the following strategy: the tone of her voice gets a little bit higher and your attention turns to her mouth and her teeth, and you forget about her hands.

Describing her makes me lazy and even somewhat melancholy. Believe me, I'd much rather think about her or remember something she did or maybe recall that day when she lost her temper and I heard a throaty voice that I would have never suspected, challenging me, her eyes full of contempt and hate and the most painful love I've ever known. Now even her memory is painful. It makes me lazy and melancholy, but let me continue: Malena's eyes are very pale. One tends to remember them as pale blue, but I would dare say they're actually rather green. One thing Malena loves to do is stare at the person who's talking to her and absorb their words with her eyes. To be clear, it's not that Malena *seems* to hear with her eyes: she does hear with her eyes, and even though she listens and doesn't say anything, her stare and the weight of her attention are so powerful that you feel interrupted, interrogated, talked about, believed, and judged by the tension of her active silence.

I remember one night in the country. Our skin was so lucid that we could feel the exact plasticity of the air. We had that full animal understanding that allows you to gain consciousness of the harmony that reality and all its levels maintain among themselves—among themselves and with us. But for my part, when I feel myself existing with that fullness, it makes me anxious, which I deal with like so: I cling to the present insanely, as if I wanted to slow down the passage of time. And then Malena, almost telepathically, asked me a question about how humans would use their time if it were up to us to decide how long a certain instant would last. Malena was like this: suddenly she'd be telling me what was happening inside my soul.

Descriptions of human beings are always partial. Partial in both senses: incomplete and self-serving. Even through their actions, it's impossible to know someone. Who knows what their motivations are, what urgency, misfortune, or transcendent nobility surrounds a given act?

Listen, we all know there are people who put off dying, some who look forward to it, others who ignore it, and more still who find it troubling. There are those who wait for it and no shortage of people who don't believe in it. Malena, however, seemed to have returned from her death and, maybe because of it, she now had the key to the world the rest of us lack. (This is all accurate, but put this way, it actually serves to obscure her because it suggests the presence of something morbid or mortal, when, in fact, the opposite is true: Malena is a fountain of life. She's one of those people who makes others feel they exist with more certainty, and even the objects around them take on a fuller existence.)

I speak with serenity and maturity, with simplicity and good sense: Malena is so full of life that she could show up here, now, suddenly, out of nowhere, and turn on the lights, talk about what she's done and whom she's seen, throw herself into my arms and inquire about something that interests her in the depths of my eyes, go to the kitchen, come back, call the grocer across the street and ask him to send over ham and Russian salad because she's hungry and there's nothing in the fridge, propose a trip while she takes off her shoes, lie down on the sofa after having turned off almost all the lights, lay her head on my chest, and take a break from life. (I'm not suggesting this could happen because of some dumb fantasy where I'm all-powerful, nor am I overly optimistic about it. I'm only saying it as a way of describing Malena, perhaps the only laudable one I've attempted. I insist: Malena can show up here, now, suddenly.)

Nothing is more tiring than love. Case in point: nobody cares how Malena feels. That is, all men care a little. But I care a lot: she walks toward an armchair until it almost touches her knees, makes a half turn on the tips of her toes without leaving the spot, and falls into a seated position with her legs crossed. It's not easy. It's another way she has of celebrating space.

Add all of this to her courage, which always leads her to choose what's most dangerous, what's least secure, what's most arduous, and what's least "reasonable," because if there's one thing that animates Malena without fail it's extending her limits to where the possible meets the impossible. (I realize this description is totally chaotic: her eyes, the way she sits, her audacity, her laughter, her agony, her hands. I'm sick of it all. If I already know what Malena's like, what's the point of this painful attempt to recreate her in words, an infinite number of which wouldn't be enough to release me for an instant from her presence.)

Where is she now? At the edge of what void? Whatever she's doing, whatever she's saying, she's always next to some kind of abyss. A painting, an idea, a voice; Malena uses them all to lead her to the edge of her own life.

Malena was delicately beautiful. She wore her life or her death with the same elegance as a beautiful dress. Arbitrary, sweet, remote. You dove into her like the sea. We learned a final form of happiness. In human terms, when things reach their end, the only thing left for them is to die. We accepted it.

I know that if I take Roigt by the scruff of his neck and throw him off this thirtieth-floor balcony and call Malena, she'll be at my home in a few minutes and we'll go back to strolling along the seafloor and the skin of the stars, and to kissing and talking about the beauty of things and the horror of death. I insist: my intuition (which has turned into faith) tells me that if I throw Roigt from the balcony, Malena will be with me tonight.

I'm not so innocent as to believe in direct causes and effects. I know that a smile in Florence can lead to a teardrop in Montevideo. I know that an unspoken word in Lima can lead to a mujik's murder. I repeat, moreover, what I have already said: Malena can appear right here, right now, suddenly, all at once.

I go to the kitchen. Roigt opens his shiny eyes. I grab him by the scruff of his neck and think again that possibly only he and I and maybe Malena are still alive. I cross the living room. I go out onto the balcony. Roigt's already hanging in the void. Underneath is the floor of the city, the skin of the world, the shell of the planet at the point where the 34th parallel and the 38th meridian intersect. If I open my hand, I'll kiss Malena today. That's all it would take: opening my right hand. The stars shine above. Next to my hand, Roigt's eyes shine, too.

Index Card

Paul Béranger (1798-1861). Critic. Béranger wrote commentary on the works of a minor poet, but his major contribution lies in the sagacity and depth of his judgment and his revolutionary views on poetry, which to some extent influenced the work of Mallarmé. Béranger died on the day he was set to be inducted into the Académie Française.

AT THE AGE OF FORTY-FIVE, Joachin Despines had published half a dozen books. His work was printed by DeGuillaume Solanger, the editor of a weekly paper with a distribution of 350 copies for readers in Ville D'Yvrex, twelve miles from Rouen. In addition to being his publisher, Solanger was Despines's loyal friend, as well as his sole and fervent admirer.

As previously stated, Despines's poetic output consisted of six books. Each received a printing of two hundred numbered editions, which were, in turn, conscientiously distributed among the greats of France. But despite this careful diffusion, the response was not what Despines had hoped for. What one might have construed to be a conspiracy of silence greeted his work, hastening its consignment to oblivion. Despines was inconsolable. His inscrutable poetry had been composed with anxiety over fame and passion for glory. Over time, a plan grew in his fighter's soul that would grant him the celebrity he so desperately craved. He sold his possessions and told Solanger he would be moving to Morocco. With tears in their eyes, they bid each other farewell.

Three months later, the editor received an apocryphal letter from Africa. It had been contrived by the poet. The letter was signed by an alleged hotelier, and claimed Despines had died from some obscure ailment. The hotelier had written to Solanger because Despines had spoken constantly of his one true friend.

The following week, Solanger dedicated his entire paper to the death of his poet friend, and, with this posthumous tribute, all of Ville D'Yvrex felt they had met their obligations to their beloved son.

But Despines, now living in Paris, went to work on his plan. He acquired the name Paul Béranger and dedicated himself to praising "France's greatest poet, Joachin Despines, born less than fifty years ago in Ville D'Yvrex, who recently died in Morocco."

The inscrutability of Despines's poems allowed him to develop an exegesis of the work and propose his own interpretations of their secret meanings. His first book of criticism, *Joachin Despines and Inscrutable Poetry*, was enthusiastically received. Béranger's second volume, *An Elucidation of the Influences at Work in the Poetry of Joachin Despines*, confirmed his genius. The giants of French literature showed up to praise him. He was awarded an honorable professorship at the university and dozens of theses were written about his literary ideas.

Béranger deployed his growing fame to shine a light on Despines's talent. Nevertheless, yet another sinister conspiracy seemed to be afoot; this time to ignore Despines and celebrate his critic.

Demoralized by his contemporaries' stubborn lack of recognition, Béranger poisoned himself the day he was set to deliver his induction speech at the Académie. Despairingly, it had been entitled *Joachin Despines: A Holy Poet*.

The translator wishes to thank the following people: Luciano Alberto, Jarrod Annis, Natalia Boquet, Julie Whelan Capell, Deborah Davidson, Lizzie Davis, Allison de-Freese, Anna Denzel, Dana Drori, Jake Eichenbaum-Pikser, Yana Ellis, Denise Fainberg, Freddie Faull, Alice Favaro, Loie Feuerle, Joaquin Goldman, Micah Hauser, Paul Holzman, Lilian Huang, Gideon Jacobs, Daniel Kaufman, Susan Kosoff, Eliana La Casa, Mark Landsman, Paul Landsman, Allie Lazar, Adam Z. Levy, Ashley Nelson Levy, Vechy Logioio, Alberto Manguel, Ghada Mourad, Karla Moyer, Betty Pérez, Rebecca Reddin, Andrea Reece, Teo Rodríguez, Jed Rothenberg, Kelly Schramm, Sydney Schutte, Sarah Schulte, Katherine Shimwell, Santiago Sorter, Carol Strauss, Jake Sugarman, Julia Tomasini, Tricia Viveros, Angela Quevado, and Samuel Weisman.

An overlooked and enigmatic master of Argentine fantastic literature, ÁNGEL BONOMINI was forty-three years old when he published *The Novices of Lerna* (1972), the first of four books of short stories he released before his death at age sixty-four. A contemporary of Jorge Luis Borges, Adolfo Bioy Casares, and Silvina Ocampo, he received the prestigious Konex Award two times.

JORDAN LANDSMAN was born in New York City. After graduating from Binghamton University, he spent several years living in Buenos Aires, where he cocreated the BA Comedy Lab. *The Novices of Lerna* is his first translation.